THE IMMERSION BOOK OF SF

THE IMMERSION BOOK OF SF

Edited by

Carmelo Rafala

IMMERSION PRESS
SUSSEX, ENGLAND, UK

THE IMMERSION BOOK OF SF

ISBN 978-0-9563924-1-1

Published in Great Britain by Immersion Press, 2010

www.immersionpress.com

INTRODUCTION

Carmelo Rafala

Living on the south coast of England has its privileges, particularly for an ex-patriot American, full-bellied on a heavy diet of speculative fiction. One could not dare to hope that, amongst the beautiful hills between Brighton and Lewis, some of the most interesting people in the genre, editors and writers alike, would be so quietly going about their lives, waiting for me to discover them.

Or maybe, they discovered me?

Let me go back a few years.

One day, not long after I moved to England to marry my lovely wife, I answered an advertisement for all *Interzone* fans to attend a final gathering with David Pringle and his original team. Suffering culture-shock, dealing with the dark British winters and looking for work, I decided that not only would I be curing my loneliness by making some new friends, but I'd be meeting people I'd admired for many years. It seemed like a win-win situation to me.

And it was.

Little did I know where such encounters and friendships would lead me. When Immersion Press was taking form with some friends in the industry, I was asked what my faviourite types of anthologies were. Did I like themed anthologies? Ones where all the stories took place in the same universe? Well, I did like those types, sure; but the ones that really stood out for me were those anthologies where each story was so vastly different from the other, that I'd felt like I'd visited a dozen or so different worlds by the time I'd put the book down.

'Perfect,' they'd said. 'You put it together.'

The terror of such a prospect floored me, speared me like a whale and dropped me to the deck of some alien sea vessel, where eager beings waited to slice me open to see what valuables I harboured in my innards. Before realising what I was in for—and probably because I hated to let my friends down—I accepted. And so I dove in, head-first, hoping to surface unscathed, treasure chest under one arm, triumphant.

What you have here—I sincerely hope—is a collection that is as varied and as entertaining as those anthologies I'd read when I was a youth. I believe that each story presented here is a world unto itself, with vistas and ideas as large and as mysterious as the universe. Since my friends approved of the selection I'd settled upon, I suppose I've succeeded.

I hope you think so, too.

Carmelo Rafala,
England, 2010

CONTENTS

THE IMMERSION BOOK OF SF

GOLDEN

Al Robertson

Outside the Museum Tavern, and I know she's inside, fresh from the East, waiting. I don't want to go in. If the whole of the city was one great pub, I could just stand here outside, and stand her up, and leave. Nothing would change.

'You said you'd be there at half past – I waited for an hour.'

'I was… I was in the bar all night long. I can't believe you didn't see me.'

Being nearby is never enough. You need to be actually present. The door opened. Someone was coming out. A snatch of conversation; 'Of course, the return on investment up there's growing all the time.'

Good to know that there were some worthwhile investments left. I pushed past them and went inside.

'So, how was Egypt?'

'Oh just lovely, it's the perfect time of year. I saw Hasem in Cairo, we were shooting at Saqqara again. He was talking about a job out there, he always does.'

I wanted to ask her about the plane journey; she hates flying. I wanted to find out if she'd been back to the Fishawi Café. We'd ended up smoking shisha there on the last night of our holiday. The tables huddled in a busy alleyway, buried deep in the Khan El-Khalili souk. Waiters scuttled between passers-by, tin trays hurtling up and down as they flew over and around heads and shoulders.

Sophie would talk to them in Arabic; she'd been learning it in night school for years. We always got excellent service. We cradled our shisha, protecting the hot coals. Heavy shopping bags bustled by, knocking against us, our rickety table. Mint tea spilled and pooled across it. We didn't really notice until it began to drip over the edge.

Most of all, I remembered the light. White charcoal smoke, winding up from a dozen shishas, condensed it from the air. Improvised streetlamps blazed; inside the café, every surface was dense with melted wax and decaying mirrors. Thick outside walls rose close around us, some hard cream, some a sticky yellow. She leaned in close to me. Her hair, her skin, her smile, were a brilliant luminous gold.

A long time ago.

'How was the flight?'

'Oh – okay…'

I'd held her hand for most of the outward flight, and for most of the return trip. She didn't like showing fear. Her grip tightened as we took off, and then again as we came in to land.

'I listened to music. There was a film.'

'You enjoyed it?'

'I didn't really get into it.'

I hated the thought of her flying alone.

*

She'd had to rush off; she had some party or other to go to. She'd promised a friend and she couldn't blow her out. She was always very particular about letting down friends. I didn't join her. I wanted to spend a bit of time just taking things in. Good things happen in the Museum Tavern; it's a lucky place. In 1941, a bomb had crashed through the roof and punched a hole in the floor by the till. It didn't detonate. Nobody had been able to work out why.

I ordered another pint, to celebrate. It was still early and I had the day's paper to finish reading. I'd kill some time, then head for home. I was part way through the G2 section when someone sat down beside me. I didn't look up. I didn't want to encourage conversation.

'Arne Hudsen'

A pause.

'I couldn't help overhearing you guys just now.'

A rich, deep, American voice – slow and measured. I kept on reading.

'I think it's great that you guys are giving it another go – you didn't see her waiting for you. Every time the door went … she'd look up, away, didn't know what to do with herself. She feels for you, son. You've done the right thing.'

I looked up from my paper, ready to shut down the conversation.

He held two tumblers, each full of whisky, catching the light like treacle.

'Son, I hate drinking on my own, too much like my old man. Scotch?'

We talked for a while. I told him a little about Sophie and me; how we'd met, how good it had been for a while, how the arguments had begun, how we'd split up. I glossed over the whole april.com thing. I didn't like talking about it much. I told him about Chris and Carticulate.

'A PR and marketing agency? Well, it's a living. I never look down on a man who makes a living for himself.'

'How about you then? A lumberjack?'

It was late; I'd had a few; Arne was built like a lumberjack. A red checked shirt stretched over his concrete-firm shoulders, hung against his squat, muscular physique. Neck like a bull's. He was an old man, maybe early 60s, but he still gave an unforced impression of power and confidence. He must have been formidable in his prime.

'A lumberjack? First time anyone said that… No, that's not me.'

'So what do you do then?'

'Well, I've retired now, thank the Lord; consult to keep ticking over, get back up there when I can. But until eight years ago I had the privilege of living upside full time and working Tranquillity moonbase as a senior mine camp commander.'

*

Next day, I was doing another new business pitch, in Reading. It was a half hour train ride from Paddington; I spent most of the journey thinking about Arne. I'd asked him some questions about the lunar mining camp, about his life in it. He'd answered calmly and in some detail. When I'd finished my drink I said goodbye and went. I think he was a bit surprised that I left so suddenly.

I'd walked down St Martin's Lane to get to the bus stop at Charing Cross station. The vacant moon hung over me. Arne was convinced that you could see the lights of some of the mining settlements from Earth, when they were in darkness. I looked up once; I didn't look up again.

When the 77A bus arrived, I made sure I couldn't see the moon from my seat.

Next day, reaching Reading and the prospect, I went straight into pitch mode. I beamed when I met him in reception; firm handshake, looked him straight in the eye. He took me into his office. There were pictures of children on his desk so I asked him about his family. I wanted him to remember a genuine connection with me.

Perhaps he was interested; in any case, he listened to me politely enough. He shook my hand at the door and gave me directions to the station.

There was nobody else around. The warehouses and offices around me looked like upside-down shoe boxes. The road between them was barely sketched in. The prospect had told me how to get out of the industrial estate. For a moment, I couldn't remember if he'd said to go left or right. I wondered if this was how Sophie imagined me spending my days.

We'd argued a lot, towards the end. Difficult times. I was out of work, didn't really believe I'd ever find anything again; april.com had crashed in early 2000. At their peak, my stock options had been worth about a million. My first proper job, after years of freelancing, and I'd made it. Sophie had glittered in my company; I thought I'd struck the motherload. We'd imagined such wonderful futures.

What a dream our life was! I took her to the best restaurants, we'd fly abroad at the drop of a hat. Once, she was working on a three week shoot in the Valley of the Queens. Her first shoot as an Assistant Producer, she'd been building up to it for years. She'd been on the phone to me a lot; it was going terribly, clashes with the director and crew. I turned up on a Friday night, surprised her, and took her down the Nile on a felucca for the weekend. I made her Cleopatra; put it all on the gold card. She'd said that it was payback for all

3

the nights and weekends I'd had to work in London.

When the company went down, there was nothing left. I wasn't even paid for my last couple of months work. I'd had to move in with her. It hadn't lasted for long. I was very angry a lot of the time. I'd wanted her to support me, she refused. We argued non-stop; split up.

I moved into a shitty one bedroom flat in Wandsworth. Chris Carter called up for the Nth time; he'd tracked me down through mutual acquaintances, the pushy bastard. This time I didn't fob him off. He wanted me to be his Strategic Development Manager, to develop new marketing strategies for Carticulate and its clients. There was nothing else on offer.

Sophie thought I was building myself up again. I wasn't so sure, but I wasn't going to let her see that. We'd started meeting up again, and things were moving on. She did most of the talking.

*

Arne was another great talker. 'God, when I think of what I had to go through – I was a test pilot for ten years before anything! And then, von Braun's tests, the fitness, all of it – they built us up for months. Now – well, you just go to Salt Lake and you're in orbit like that, then wherever you want. Son, you got it easy – go for it!'

I'd bump into him every few days, sometimes have a scotch or a couple of pints with him. He wasn't sure if he liked the Museum Tavern; but had said at least it felt like he was really getting away when he went there. I didn't like it when he talked about the moon. He also believed that the Germans had helped set up Israel in the late 30s ('That's why they didn't make a fuss when we poached von Braun – we were putting far too much money into all that for them to say no'). He didn't seem to know much about the Second World War either. Apart from that, he was pretty good company.

I'd been moaning about work; Chris was getting me down. He didn't seem to understand what I could do for him.

'Lex, I'll level with you. I don't know why you're still here. You could be in the industry, running a portal; bright guy like you, they'd love you topside. You could be running trades on the mine sites – Lord knows, they need all the help they can get, and they've got money to burn. My God! There's so much up there – and you'd be making a killing, that's for sure.'

Arne was convinced. He'd planned a future for me. I'd dump Carticulate, use my dotcom experience to get into space. Once there, I'd achieve my potential, make my fortune and that would be it. I let him talk for a bit, and then I changed the subject. I knew there was no topside; but, if nothing else, his optimism was infectious.

Talking to Arne always cheered me up; he was much more together than you'd have thought. He told me a lot about his family. He was over in London visiting his daughter, who'd just had her first baby. He'd come over with his wife to help out, for a month or two. Every so often it all got a bit much for him, so he'd pop out for a walk and a drink. Back then, I was surprised that they trusted him to look after himself; I never saw any of them with him.

*

I didn't spend too long with him that night. I had an early start the next day, going to Bath for another pitch. I didn't fancy waiting for a bus, so I got the tube south from Tottenham Court Road.

The carriage was quite full. I couldn't get a seat so I stood by the door. I was thinking about Carticulate; Arne had inspired me. If I wasn't happy there, it wasn't necessarily a problem. I could change it.

Two men were talking behind me. I was half listening to the conversation. Their investment chat mixed in with my thoughts about Chris. I heard them mention mining. One of them seemed to be talking about the moon, and then Mars.

The train was juddering into Leicester Square station. I stumbled as I began to turn round, knocking into someone. By the time I'd apologised we were in the station. The men I'd overheard had got out. There were several people walking down the platform towards the exit. I couldn't tell which ones they were. The doors closed again, and we moved on.

*

I got back from Bath and went straight to meet Sophie. We were still getting used to being together again. She'd badger me to tell her what I was up to at Carticulate. I'd give her the positive version.

She was waiting at the NFT Bar, nursing a glass of white wine. Outside, the booksellers were just packing up for the day. She'd said she had some exciting news, but she seemed quite down. I told her about Bath, that it had gone well.

'Lex, look – I talked to Hasem today.'

'Great – how is he?'

'He's fine – but he's offered me a job – he wants me to go to Cairo full time, be a liaison for crews over there, develop some ideas with him.'

'Oh.'

'Lex, this is what I've always dreamed of.'

'I know. You're going to take it?'

*

In Bath, I'd thought I'd seen a billboard advertising holidays in space. I was in a cab, heading for the prospect; we were moving too fast for me to read it properly. On the way back to the station, the cabbie had taken me down the same road. Looking up, I could only see pictures of some sort of soap.

*

Next day, I sat down with Chris for our weekly sales update. There wasn't much to report. I was cold calling people from his contact database. Most of them were polite but uninterested. Some promised to keep our details. Hardly any wanted to meet and talk.

'What do you mean, you want me to keep calling these losers? We should be in new markets! This is the wrong time to talk to these guys. Technology's crashed; no-one's spending. We need to be moving into new sectors. We need to be somewhere booming.'

Chris hated me telling him how to run his business, but I was right about this, so I pushed.

'Okay, Lex, if you feel that strongly about it – look into it, do me a report or something. But I don't want it getting in the way of new business, it's not really what I took you on for.'

I bit my tongue; I'd got what I wanted.

'To be honest, Lex, I'm a bit disappointed with things. Do what you want; but make sure you get some more leads. That's important, that's what you're here for.'

*

The next time I saw Arne he was a bit less cheerful than normal. I asked him if he was okay; he said yes; I left it at that. I steered the conversation towards his days in space. He loved talking about his past; I thought it might cheer him up. I was also very curious. I wanted to know more about his world. It sounded so exciting.

'Remember my first time topside, it was '71. One of six missions; climbed out of the lander, stood there, looked up at the Earth. My God! All that time on another planet. Sure, there were experiments, all that, but hell – they were make time things. Important thing – we were there; we could get there. We were living dreams back then.'

'Went up another two, three times in the early 70s – budgets low while they put money into Vietnam, reparations, proper democracy now. Spent a lot of time going round schools, bright-eyed kids – I'd always take quarters with me, ones I'd taken to the moon. Hand 'em out as prizes to the smart ones, the ones with the stars in their eyes.'

I let him talk on. By the mid-90s, the moon was pretty much commercialised, he was consulting for some of the bigger private mining firms, living more and more off share income. He'd struck gold, got in at the start with some of the biggest names out there; now he never needed to work again.

Arne's life reminded me of the future I'd shared with Sophie – only work when I wanted to, consulting internationally, follow her round the world, let her track me as I went off exploring. We were going to spend months in Egypt – going down the Nile, living in Cairo, she'd make films, I'd write a book, read, whatever.

Arne's conviction was absolute. He had walked in space, and had worked professionally on the moon for five years or more. He showed me the vacuum blossoms on his gut, where his suit had been penetrated by a micro-meteorite, nearly sucking him into the void; he showed me a tiny slab of moonrock that he'd had made into a keyring. He even talked about how much money Carticulate could make if it picked up a few industry contracts.

They called last orders at the bar. Hardly any time seemed to have passed. Arne stopped me as I stood up to get the last round in.

6

'Son, there's something I'm going to say to you. I'll say it once, and that'll be it.'

He was looking at me intently.

'When I come here, it's different. I look round, people aren't happy, the stars don't shine bright enough. I know, I've spent my life watching 'em. This isn't a good place for a young man to be, son, you've got to get while the going's good and move. You don't want to waste your life in shitty places like this.'

*

On my way home, something caught my eye – the cover of a magazine in the newsagent's window. It was that week's edition of Time. It showed two men in bulky pressure suits standing in a bleak, red tinged landscape. The suits' visors were mirrored; you couldn't see their faces. They reflected a camera, some buildings, distant red mountains. One of them was hefting a pickaxe, the other was holding a briefcase. A headline ran beneath them. It read 'MARS - OPEN FOR BUSINESS'.

*

'You seem very bouncy.'

Sophie was very good at picking up my moods.

'You're almost manic. What's got into you?'

I had a new world inside me. The newsagent had denied all knowledge of that edition of Time when I went back; I hadn't been able to find it anywhere else. That wasn't important. I'd seen it, had stood staring at it, hands pressed against the cold glass, reading that single, simple sentence over and over again. It had been real. A world of miracles had started to blossom.

'Oh, I just want to take advantage of you while you're still here, I don't want to waste a second. Come on!'

A Sunday afternoon on Clapham Common; the air fresh with the first rush of spring. Everything seemed to be possible. Sophie was glowing again; overjoyed by the job, overjoyed to be with me. We took off across the Common running, thrilled. Everything was fantastic.

On our way up Clapham High Street we'd stopped at a pine furniture shop. Sophie was looking for a new bed; she was going to rent her flat out while she was abroad, and needed to turn her study into a second bedroom. I'd pottered round in the background while she haggled with the owner.

Pine furniture shops smell so distinctive; that sweet scent, oozing from everything. I ran my hand along the end of a bed, the side of a cupboard. The wood was sticky, rich with sap. The afternoon sun gilded it, dancing on luminous surfaces. It warmed me as Sophie turned towards me, her face alive with joy as she prepared for her move to the South.

On the Common, she fell into my arms. I felt the heavy, perfect weight of her as she pulled me over too, dense as an ingot, dragging down my heart. We rolled in the grass and I kissed her, her small mouth fiery and hot to the tongue. I felt my stubble rasp across her pale skin, igniting it. Her hair was a golden blaze around her head; her blue eyes burned like the sky where it flew closest to the sun.

'My God I could love you so much.'

Some kind of heaven.

*

I didn't spend the whole night with her; I had an early start. I was going to Slough to talk to some clients about re-branding their travel booking system. I hadn't really prepared much for the meeting, but I was on such a high that I didn't really care. I decided to walk home.

The Common opened itself up to receive me, then enfolded me in soft darkness. I passed the bandstand, kept on walking down the fur-grey path. A cloud shifted; suddenly everything around me was buttered with moonlight.

To my left, black trees in pubic clumps, thick and knotted. A friend went cottaging in there, from time to time. A government minister had been caught out round here, chasing fantasies into the headlines. He'd fallen. I think he now held obscure political office in Wales.

The path leads straight to the road; you come out of the darkness, into the sodium gash of pavement light. A zebra crossing; a bus is coming. I wait, let it shudder past. Look up at the top deck, then, as it breaks out of cloud, at the moon.

It's a half moon; one side soft cream, the other rich with shadow. Light stipples the velvet dark, thick white pricks rained across the black. I recognise the shimmering patterns that Arne has so carefully described: the Silent Fist, the Smiling Cat, the Nickel and Dime, the Others.

New constellations have landed on the moon; all of Arne's moon camps are there. Everything's changed, for good. I'd followed Arne away from the Museum Tavern, away from the dead roads of Holborn and the darkness of that other, hopeless London. I'd taken his advice; I'd got out. Now, I stood beneath a moon spattered with mines, a moon that was pumping the Earth full of wealth. I could rebuild myself on my share of that wealth. I'd broken through, and I would see that breakthrough infect my job, my life, my world.

*

I never saw Arne again.

He'd told me that he'd had enough of Holborn and wanted to start meeting somewhere else – somewhere a little closer to his daughter's place. It was on the other side of the Thames, in Southwark. The pub was called the Queen of Hearts.

I still remember the excitement of that journey. I decided to walk. I had an hour or so to kill, and I needed the exercise. I went south to the Thames and then crossed over to the South Bank. It was a cloudy night. I couldn't see the moon, but I was confident that the new lights that spilled across it would still be shining. The world around me was imminent with the golden age of space, with its newly fertile presence.

I couldn't find the Queen of Hearts. The street was narrow, red terraced houses cramped hard against each other, squashed shoulder to shoulder. The

8

pub should have been halfway down. Instead, there was a small, modern block of flats, all grey concrete and dull, flat planes. I stopped a couple of people and asked them for directions, but nobody could help.

*

Sophie moved to Egypt soon afterwards. I went to the airport with her to say goodbye. I watched the plane lift off into the bright open sky from the car park. For once, she hadn't been nervous of flying. She was too excited. I think Chris had sacked me by then.

I'd felt Arne's disappearance as a personal failure. Perhaps I had written the address of the pub down wrong. One day, I broke off from writing my report and went onto the internet. I spent hours trying to track it down. There had once been a Queen of Hearts in Bear Lane. It had been bombed flat during the Blitz.

*

I am still researching my report. I know that, if I write it well enough, it will reopen the doors that have been closed to me. I've mapped out the economic benefits of investing in the new space operations in some detail. I've explored their workings: the minimum workforce necessary to support profitable mining operations, the need for a magnetic rail gun to shoot processed ore from the lunar surface back to Earth, and so on.

Working with the new materials from space, and the new industries needed to service the men mining those materials, we can create a new business paradigm that will revolutionise the economic world. All will be set in a cycle of perpetual profit. New markets will fuel constant economic growth. We shall live effortlessly in a golden age, greater than any that's been seen before.

I am paying my rent with a new credit card. It will be good for another few months. I live frugally. I believe in the world I am looking for. When I am not writing I walk the streets of London, searching for it. I am committed and determined in my search, for I know it can be found. The moon will light up for me again; I shall count the returning shuttles as they drop like coins from the sky.

I have made a list of the sites of other pubs that were destroyed in World War II. In that other world, I believe that they survived. I go to them, one by one. Searching for Arne revealed nothing. A young test pilot with the same name had been killed in a car crash in the late 50s. There was nothing else.

Sophie sent me a letter the other day. She told me how exciting life was in Cairo, how happy she was to be out there. Hasem is a well connected man; she's mixing with the highest levels of Egyptian society. She recently appeared in the pages of their version of Hello. The woman behind the counter at her grocers had recognised her and been very impressed. Sophie was overjoyed. I spoke to my mother a few weeks ago; she said she'd heard from her as well.

I have not told her that I am no longer working for Carticulate. She thinks that I am spearheading an expansion into new business areas. I am not lying to her. When I find that other world again, I shall be a wealthy man. I cannot

9

afford to visit her now. I tell her I am too busy. She understands, and doesn't pressure me.

There are roads on my list that I've not yet been to; one by one, I'm visiting them all. Some day I shall turn into one and find, in place of a drab fifties housing block or a grey, concrete shopping precinct, an old London pub bustling with life and energy. I shall walk into it, and Arne will be sitting at the bar, waiting for me. We will talk again about the future, and the past, and both will be glowing with promise and reward.

*

Before she left, Sophie took me to Hampton Court Palace. She said she wanted to take me away from it all for an afternoon. I'd told her a little about Arne, but not the full story. Perhaps I'd been wrong not to do so. I'd been drawn into his world by his stories. Maybe they would act as a door for her as well. I tried to tell her about his life on the moon, but she changed the subject.

Later that afternoon, I caught her looking at me in a peculiar way, somewhere between appraisal and concern. I could understand how she was feeling. We were exploring the maze together. So many narrow green pathways, all confusingly the same. It was so easy to take the wrong turning, so difficult to know which was right. In the end, she let me lead. I'd told her I knew my way around.

We suddenly stumbled on the central area. I'd seen a film, several years ago, in which the hero and heroine had had a picnic there. There had been a small garden: regularly planted trees, rich flower beds at the feet of the hedges, enclosing an elegant central lawn. It was a little piece of paradise.

When we arrived, there was only an empty, muddy quadrangle.

I said, 'I told you I knew where it was.'

Two sickly trees leant against each other like stubbed out cigarettes. The sky was heavy and cold above the drab green hedges. The blank white moon had appeared, foreshadowing darkness. I stood alone with Sophie at the maze's cold heart, wondering how I'd managed to find it. For a moment I even wanted to tell her that I didn't know how to get out.

TAN

Tanith Lee

All afternoon she lay, her pale body soaking up the sun on the hill. It was July, and hot, and she had always tanned easily—when she could make time for it. Where sunlamps turned her yellow, genuine light dyed her golden.

She had been very careful to select a venue that was utterly private. No one lived inside six miles. The woods began at least one mile below. Here there wasn't a tree or bush. Only the mat of flattened summer grass to lie in. She knotted up her hair as well, before slipping off her clothes. The tan had to be perfect. Tonight he was taking her to the special club, to drink champagne cocktails and dance. She had had the dress two weeks. It was sheer black, sleeveless yet fairly modest from the front, though fitting her closely. But the back dipped low. She had a good body, and he liked it a lot. When brown, (gold) she would *shine*.

The place—the hill—she had known about since her youth, all of five years before. She had come up there once or twice, driven in a boyfriend's car. But others sometimes came there as well, then for different reasons. The hill was a favourite from which to spot UFOs. She herself didn't believe in flying saucers, or if there were any, why on earth (ha!) would they come near earth? One of her evening companions on the hill did point out a moving light above. But she told him it must be a plane. After she had grown up and gone away to get rich in the city, she heard that on a cloudy November night, a strange fiery object had been seen falling on the hill top. The crash and flash, the local newspapers had reported, had been heard, felt and seen across ten counties. But when police, ambulance and fire crew finally made it up the hill, nothing was to be found. "It was as if," one agitated witness later announced, "the doomed craft plunged straight through the fabric of the ground, alter-dimensionally leaving barely any evidence of its doubtless terminal descent."

The hill, now designated the 'Tomb of Unknown Friends from Another

World', had for a while been much SF-geeked over. But no longer. Indeed, people seemed now to avoid the place.

About two o'clock, satisfied with her frontal tones, she turned over on to her face. She knew that in this position she might fall asleep, so prudently set the alarm on her phone for four. By then she would be the cake that angels baked.

She wasn't wrong about sleeping. After ten minutes she began to doze. She let go and slid down into a warm oblivion, where only once a peculiar dream half woke her, but afterwards she couldn't really recall why. It had something to do with crying voices, she thought, when the alarm fully roused her. Voices—and someone reaching out to her. It was not a pleasant dream. It had a sort of edge of panic to it, a weird, ill-defined frisson of resentful anger, and pain.

She shook it off quickly, of course, and by the time she was down the hill and driving back to town, she had thoughts only for the way he was going to look at her when she showed herself to him in the new dress and the new tan.

*

He arrived a little too early. She liked his eagerness, but would have preferred she had been ready. Even so, a glimpse in the shower, before steam obscured it, had already shown her how beautifully her legs, breasts and arms had toasted. So she donned the dress and came out, and having seen his face, turned slowly around to show him the back of her. Though she hadn't yet seen herself like this, she could well imagine. She anticipated his speechlessness, or extreme praise, perhaps even an interruption before she could finish her make-up. The one thing she did *not* expect was—

"Why are you laughing?" she demanded, spinning to confront him, startled and, well, frankly unnerved.

"God, you haven't seen, have you? What did you do, fall asleep under a *tree?*"

"What—do you mean?" She stared at him. "Obviously I would *never* try to tan under a tree—"

Briskly—she had never liked his *briskness*—he directed her to return into the bedroom. "Get a mirror and take a look at your back. God!" He laughed again. "You're dumb. Go on, go and see. And then change your bloody dress, for God's sake."

She went into the other room and slammed the door. She took off the dress and grabbed a hand mirror. Standing with her back to the long mirror on the wall, she looked to see what he had found fault with. Until that minute she was thinking he had either gone mad, or was winding her up because he secretly disliked her.

In the mirror then. In the mirror.

Her back was a canvas of flawless golden flesh, across which there spread, where the sun had been statically blocked off from her for two solid hours, a lattice-work of white, untanned skin. This clearly depicted a tangle of stretching, clawing, agonized, terrified and pleading, tiny little three-fingered hands.

HAVE GUITAR, WILL TRAVEL

Chris Butler

A-Side

I sheltered in a doorway, trying to hide from a cold January wind so I could smoke a cigarette. I heard footsteps, noticed the polished shine of the guy's shoes, but I didn't look up. "I just want a few minutes on my own," I said.

"I'm not looking for an autograph, Ray," the man said. "I have a message for you."

I did look up then, and my reward was a flash of light that blinded me. *Paparazzi*, I thought. Not that they were hounding me lately, but you live in hope. I heard a car door slam. When I could see again the street was empty.

In my hand I held a business card, but how I came to be holding it I didn't know. It read:

GARR-DAVIS MESSAGE SERVICES
— From the far colonies to the inner worlds —
Memetic Incursion a speciality

I turned the card over. There didn't seem to be any message. *Bizarre*, I thought. I looked up into the night sky, and saw a flash from the jump gate orbiting far above. Maybe some day I'd get to tour the far colonies. Have guitar, will travel. But I was strictly inner worlds so far.

I couldn't see a litterbin nearby. That's England for you, right shit-hole. So I put the card in my pocket. Back inside the club I could hear the crowd still clapping, calling for another encore, but I'd given them enough for one night.

The wind gusting up from the seafront rattled some loose railings nearby. I only had a thin jacket on over a t-shirt, and I was cold. I headed down Abbey in the direction of The Golden Grill — the all-day breakfast bar. The band would know to look for me there. I could never eat before a gig, but I'd be starving hungry later.

*

The doorbell jingle-jangled as I went inside the glittering palace that is The Golden Grill. There were a couple of other customers in, but they were getting ready to leave. Jane looked at me as I sat down on a stool at the front counter.

"It's me," I said.

"So it is. I heard you were in town." Jane Monet had beautiful skin and a wide smile. "Don't you have no place else to go?"

"You wait on tables, I sit on stools."

She looked at me like she'd seen something move at the corner of her eye. "Is that a line from a song?" she asked.

"Something I'm working on," I said. "Probably nothing."

She laughed and asked me what I wanted to eat. I just wanted coffee for now. I'd order food when the guys caught up with me. I watched the easy movement of her body as she turned, the nonchalant sway of her hips. I'd love to dance with her some time. She mumbled something about needing refills for the coffee machine and went to the storeroom out back.

I took the business card from my pocket and studied it again. Then I heard a voice, a familiar but completely unexpected voice. She said, "It's been a while, Ray."

She was dressed in jeans and a thick woollen jumper, and she was sitting on the stool next to me. "Chloe?"

Then I noticed distortions and imperfections in the image. It was high definition, but not as good as the real thing.

She said, "Wouldn't it be something if Chloe was really here."

I couldn't stop staring and my heart was hammering in my chest. Then the words 'Memetic Incursion' came back to me. Jane had come back with a bag of coffee. I asked, "Is there a business card in my hand?" I held it up. She looked confused and shook her head. "And there's no one sitting next to me, is there?"

The Chloe-image said, "You shouldn't take candy from strangers, Ray."

"I never took anything from anyone," I said.

Jane came closer. "What are you talking about? No, there's no one sitting next to you."

"Shit."

Memetic incursion. I hadn't heard of it before but it probably meant what it sounded like: some kind of virus software running loose in my mind. It would cost to get it cleared out. I knew a guy, Johnny Tag, who could help me. Johnny stayed on top of this sort of thing. About a year before, he erased some Mapper's Delight I carelessly acquired from dodgy company at an after-gig party.

Jane frowned. "Are you okay?"

"Looks like I've been infected with a memetic avatar of my ex-girlfriend. We're having a conversation. Not much of one though."

14

"Oh, right," Jane said. "Bummer."

"Just ignore us. I mean, me. I'd still like that coffee. Do you have a pen I can use?"

I turned to 'Chloe'. "Why are you here?" I asked.

"Maybe to give you some closure," she replied.

I smiled in that way you do when you stub your toe. "That would be nice," I said. But the truth is I didn't need closure from Chloe. I was over her long ago. If I needed closure from anyone I needed it from Maia Laine, my most recent disaster. But even that ranked lower than the idea of starting something with the lovely Jane Monet, who had gone back to brewing coffee.

"I saw one of your concerts recently," Chloe said. "Not live, I imported it. You're still singing 'Counting The Days'. You still look like you mean it."

I shrugged. "It's a good song, a crowd-pleaser."

"Maybe it is, but I don't think that's why you still sing it. You still think that somewhere down the line we're going to get back together. You think you're going to come back home one day and I'll be there waiting for you. It's not going to happen, Ray."

Good, I thought, marvelling at her self-delusion. Jane handed me a pen. I reached for a napkin and wrote down Johnny Tag's name and address. "And yet here you are," I said to Chloe.

"After a fashion," Chloe said. "Get ready, Ray, we're going on a journey. Say goodbye to your friend."

I handed the napkin to Jane. "Look after me when I'm gone."

Jane folded her arms and looked at me like I was a kid gone bad. "Gone?"

"I'm going to be out of my head for a while. If I start drooling, try to get hold of this guy, Johnny Tag. He might be able to help me."

Her expression softened and she nodded.

In that moment I realized she could be important to me. We could be good for each other, but we had never talked about it. Stupid. "Your eyes are brown," I told her. "Did you know mine are blue?"

She frowned and squinted her eyes. "Must you always..."

But I didn't hear the end of it. I felt light-headed, and she seemed very far away. I never did get the coffee.

*

I woke to the sound of feet thumping against the floorboards of the room above, turned over, and pulled a pillow over my head. It was dark in the room, but I knew where I was: Theresa's Bed & Breakfast. Then I remembered that I shouldn't be, that I hadn't been there in years.

The smell of bacon wafted up from the kitchen downstairs. I got out of bed and went to the window. It must have been raining earlier; there were pools of water in the garden. Theresa's garden had bad drainage. I found some clothes in a drawer, and on the bedside cabinet there was a half-full pack of cigarettes. I dressed and went downstairs to the dining room.

Theresa came in from the kitchen. "Morning, Mr Chase," she said. "Full English breakfast for you?"

There were no other guests about. I stared at her, puzzled. This was Chloe's mum, but she was acting like we barely knew each other. "Yes please," I said. I hadn't made it as far as eating anything in The Golden Grill and I was starving.

She came back with a plate piled high with food: bacon, sausage, hash browns, eggs, mushrooms, tomatoes and a rack of toast. I reached for the brown sauce and added some to my plate.

"Is there anything else you need?" she asked, smiling.

I always used to take a walk in the garden after breakfast. Theresa didn't allow smoking indoors. "Do you mind if I go out back when I've finished?" I waved the cigarette packet at her.

"Go ahead. It's not so nice out though. Summer's about over, I think."

Last I knew, it was January. Deep into winter. This couldn't be real, but I ate the breakfast anyway. Then I went outside and ambled down the path through the garden. I lit a cigarette and inhaled deeply. Theresa had a grapevine growing against an old, neglected greenhouse. I examined the grapes and saw that they were ripe, so it seemed to be late summer like she said.

I heard footsteps and turned around. Chloe was walking down the path towards me. It all made sense to me then. This moment was one of my most vivid memories. She wore a white and blue dress and Wellington boots.

"Hello, Ray," she said.

I said, "I wrote 'Breakfast Smoke' here."

She held up a hand to shield her eyes from the sun rising over the neighbouring gardens. "You're such a shit, Ray. I don't know what I ever saw in you."

"What?" This wasn't what happened before. I'd had a couple of hit records by then, and some press attention. She was thrilled to meet me and we hit it off straight away.

She said, "This moment was the first time we met, but all you care about is that you wrote a song here."

I put the cigarette to my lips.

"Filthy habit," she remarked.

I shook my head wearily. "This isn't the way it happened. You're changing it."

"You were an opportunity. A chance for me to get out of this crummy place."

I stared at her. "That is not true. You weren't like that."

She scoffed. "How would you know what I was like? You were always lost in your own head, too involved with your image, too surrounded by sycophants to know how anyone honestly felt about anything. And you haven't changed a bit."

"You sound like Maia," I noted.

"Who?"

"After your time," I said. "My most recent girlfriend. She said I was self-absorbed."

"I like her already," Chloe said.

In an instant, my world went dark again.

Then an explosion of light and I was gasping for breath back at The Golden Grill all-day breakfast bar. I saw Jane staring down at me with a worried expression on her face.

"Did you call Johnny Tag?" I managed to ask between deep breaths.

"Give us a chance," Jane said. "You keeled over and you haven't moved for the last minute. I didn't think you were breathing."

My pulse was racing and I was sweating like a pig. "Looks like … this avatar in my head is … taking me on trips into my memories. Call Johnny Tag now. No, wait, it will take too long. I can't believe it's only been a minute. I..."

Darkness again.

*

I pulled the straps from her shoulders and the dress fell to the floor. I took my shirt off, held Chloe close and kissed her. She pushed me back onto the bed and sat in my lap, pulled her head back and gazed lovingly into my eyes.

She brushed forward and back against me and said, "I'm not really into this, you know."

What?

She said, "This is a memory from a year later. You think we're happy but I had a lot of problems already. I was just going through the motions, pretending, because I didn't want to hurt you. You didn't notice though."

I pushed her off. "No, no, you're not that good an actress, you never did that. You're re-writing history."

She rolled over on the bed, pulled her knees up and stretched an arm under her head for a pillow. "You can enter Chloe's memories if you want. If you really want to know what was happening to her. Her memories are replicated inside this image."

I stared at her. Not knowing what really happened to Chloe was the hardest thing. One day she was here, the next she had gone. I mean, she left a note, but it didn't really say *why*.

"This is your only chance, Ray. If you want to know Chloe's story, you have to say now."

Damn. I really thought I was over all this. "Yes," I conceded. "Yes, I want to know."

"This might take a minute," the Chloe-image said.

She let me go again, back to Jane's bar. The real world hit me like a vice tightening. Every muscle ached. From what I could make out, I wasn't breathing during these flashbacks.

"Ray," Jane said, "you're scaring me."

I figured I could only stand so many of these episodes. So I was scared too.

"We're going into her memories next... Maybe there is time … after all … to get Johnny Tag down here..."

"I called him," she said.

The lights above us seemed incredibly bright. Then the scene changed again.

17

*

The woman leaned forward and smiled. "If you'd like to follow me," she said. I tried to look around, but I seemed to have no control over my body. I stood up and followed her into an office, where she introduced me as Miss Chloe Hart.

Johnny Tag stood up from behind his desk and came to shake her hand. I hadn't realized they even knew each other. *When was this?*

Johnny always looked like he was freezing cold, thanks to a lack of pigment in his skin. You'd think he'd smile more to make up for it. "Please sit down," he said. "What can I do for you, Chloe?"

She fidgeted nervously. "I think I'm infected with something. Mapper's Delight maybe."

"Nasty stuff," Johnny said. Too right. MapperD runs through your head like a mischievous devil, giving you reckless ideas and making them seem rational. Without treatment, people tend not to live long. "Been mixing with the wrong crowd, have you?"

"I guess so," Chloe said, and shrugged.

Was this before I had my own problem with MapperD? I remembered now how quickly Johnny Tag's name had come up back then.

"Well I can help you, of course I can," Johnny assured her, "but I don't work for free."

Chloe bit her lip. "My boyfriend is Ray Chase. I can get some money."

Johnny waved his hand dismissively. "I don't want your money."

"Oh," she said.

"And don't worry, I'm not looking to pull your knickers down either. No offence, but I've seen better looking girls."

I could feel Chloe's heart racing in her chest. "Then what?"

"Ray Chase, you say. I heard about Ray Chase. I heard he only records a tenth of what he writes."

"That's true, he says you have to be careful about over-exposure. Just use the best. But what has that got to do with...?"

"That's a whole lot of other songs lying around doing nothing. I bet he sings them songs to you, long before he gets anywhere near a recording studio."

"Sometimes he does."

"So, if I let some spiders loose in your head, they can cull recordings from your memories."

I remembered when spiders looked like spiders. *Johnny Tag, you bastard.*

"That is so illegal," Chloe said. Too right it is.

"What are you going to do?" Johnny asked. "Log negative feedback against me?"

"I could report you to the Memory Protection Agency. Ray knows his way around the legal side of the music business. He says the MPA is like a dog after a bone. Maybe they could cull some evidence from my memories."

Mention of the MPA made me feel even more uncomfortable. Maia Laine, my most recent girlfriend, works for the MPA. But that didn't seem to be relevant to anything I was seeing here. At least, I hoped not. I'd had dealings with the MPA as long as I'd been making music. I always paid my membership fees. A lot of bootlegging goes on, despite everyone's best efforts. Some of it is tolerated, but if you're really being ripped off the MPA will fight for you.

Johnny nodded slowly. "Maybe they could. But, well, I haven't actually done anything yet. I was just speaking in the hypothetical. And in the meanwhile, you still have a head full of MapperD."

"Someone else could help me with that."

"Sure. But look, no one needs to know anything about this. I'm talking about selling bootlegs on distant colonies, far from here. Ray will never know. I realize how much trouble I'd be in if the MPA traced this stuff to me, so I'm not going to push it on my own doorstep."

She looked at him for a long while. Then she said, "How about if I get a percentage of the profits?"

What?

Johnny smiled. "I think we can do business."

"Okay then," Chloe said.

I couldn't believe it. How easily and quickly she'd sold me out. Was this the girl I'd wanted so desperately to find again?

Maybe it was the MapperD that did this to her? I remembered the brief period when I was infected. I almost took a flight off the roof of a building. I almost drowned. I almost overdosed on more conventional drugs.

The scene froze, like a recording that had reached its end. Then I was gasping for air again, my chest heaving. I tried to focus on Jane's concerned face.

"God, Ray. I'm scared for you. Make it stop."

"Just … need … catch my breath... Don't think she's … finished with me yet..."

"That guy, Johnny Tag, he's coming down here. I hope he can help you."

I knew now that I couldn't trust Tag, but there was no time to explain. The Chloe mind-ware pulled me back into another memory.

*

A memory of mine, this time. We were in the bedroom. Looked like one of our lazy Sunday mornings. I was sitting cross-legged on the bed, holding an acoustic. I watched her, my gaze tracing the curve of her shoulders.

She propped a pillow behind her head. "Sing 'East End Basket Case' for me, Ray."

I searched for the chords and hummed a little of the melody. It would be easy to give in to the illusion, but Chloe didn't lie in the sheets of my bed any more.

"No, no," she said, playfully poking her toe at me. "Sing it like you mean it."

I would have too. I never recorded the song; I thought it was too personal. It was supposed to be just for her. Supposed to be.

"You were just using me," I said.

She frowned. "So now you know, Ray. Those last few months, I was soaking up those songs whenever I could get you to sing them to me. Then I gave them all to Johnny Tag."

I threw the guitar aside. It struck the wall and clattered to the floor and rang painfully. The avatar kept placing us in these scenarios pulled from memory, but it was all changed. I struggled to find my bearings.

I said, "Am I popular then? In the outermost colonies? Big-in-Japan without ever knowing?"

She sat up, holding the sheet around her. Suddenly she looked less defiant and more sad. "How would I know? Ask Johnny Tag."

I searched her face. "I thought you went into business with him."

She laughed coldly. "He dealt with the MapperD, I was a liability with that running round my head, but he never had any intention of giving me any of the money. Why should he? He had me squirming on the hook, right where he wanted me. He had no reason to do anything for me."

"So he just fucked you over," I said.

"You and me both," she answered.

I held onto that thought as I got another fleeting glimpse of Jane, back in the real world.

"Johnny Tag just called from a taxi," Jane said. "He'll be here soon."

I grimaced with the pain in my chest. I figured I better stay alive long enough to give Johnny the greeting he deserved.

*

When Chloe left me, she left a note behind. It said she didn't love me any more. I remember holding the note in my hand. I couldn't hold it steady and I couldn't put it down.

Now I saw her write the note. It didn't seem to bother her much. Then she went to the port and got in line, ID clutched in sweaty hand, just the one bag slung over her shoulder.

"I did everything Johnny asked," she said as she shuffled forward. New words superimposed on old actions again. "I let him take all your songs. I thought that would be the end of it, but he didn't just want your back catalogue. He wanted me to stay close to you; he wanted everything you would ever write."

She kept moving up toward the security gate. I walked alongside her, as I never had in reality. I tilted my head up and saw the starlit sky above, glistening beyond the transparent shield. There was a flash from the jump gate every minute or so, a lot of people moving through.

She said, "I stole your money, Ray. Emptied out the joint account you set up for us. I'm sorry about that, but I had to be free of Johnny Tag."

"Am I supposed to feel sorry for you?"

She shook her head. "Some days I think it was all my fault; I had something good and I personally fucked it up. Other days I think I never had a

20

chance. Maybe it was Johnny who slipped me the MapperD in the first place."

She showed her ID at the gate and went through.

First a shuttle, then the jump gate.

Soon she'd be far away.

*

I can't remember much of the months after Chloe left, but I guess it's all in my head somewhere. She found something more to torment me with.

"Who's this, Ray?" she asked, her voice like acid, "and how old is she?"

Chloe stood next to the bed I was in. The curtains were closed. I looked away from her and saw the girl lying beside me: slim build, straight black hair. She turned over in her sleep. "It's Maia," I said. Maia Laine, my latest girl-friend. But something wasn't quite right here. Maia looked younger than she was when we got together. But she wasn't underage or anything like that. What was going on here? Was Chloe messing with my memories again?

Presumably not, because Chloe looked pissed that I knew the girl's name. "Maybe you're not the complete jackass I thought you were," she said.

"There were a lot of girls after you left," I replied.

"Yes, a lot. Sifting through your memories has been quite an unpleasant task."

"You're not even her."

"I'm an image of her. I know how she felt."

"What does she want from me? Why have you done all of this?"

"Chloe wants you to stop singing 'Counting The Days', Ray. That song says you put your life on hold, just waiting till you could get back with her. She's not worth it. She screwed you over and you're better off without her."

"You've got it all wrong," I said. "It's just a song. What is it you really want? It seems like you just want to tarnish every memory I have of her."

She took a step back, almost vanishing in the dark of the room. "I think we're just about done here."

I nearly felt sad about it.

"There's just one more thing I want you to do for me," she said.

*

I climbed unsteadily to my feet, Jane helping me up.

"I think I'll be all right now," I said, and held her close. Then the room started to spin around me so I sat down on a chair.

"I'll get you some water," Jane said.

I'd sat at a messy table. Jane hadn't cleared away the last customer's plates and cutlery. There was a steak-knife. I could still see Chloe, sitting on the stool over by the front counter, watching me.

The front door of The Golden Grill jingle-jangled and I saw Johnny Tag coming in. I glanced at Chloe and she looked like she had a sour taste in her mouth.

I forced myself up onto my feet as Johnny came over. "Heard you were in trouble," Johnny said. "Picked up some bad shit?"

21

"Yes," I replied. Over Tag's shoulder I could see the front door opening again. The rest of my band had arrived. They were laughing and joking with each other as they came in.

I learned later that I picked up the steak-knife and stabbed Tag in the chest with it. I have no memory of that. Not then, not later, but there were plenty of witnesses who saw me do it.

I just remember this puzzled expression on his face, then he staggered back and fell, knocking over some stools. And there was this really horrible gurgling sound as his last breath escaped.

"Oh my God, Ray!" Jane cried. "What have you done?"

B-Side

A lawyer came to see me. He wore an expensive suit. I could smell peaches on him, and boot polish. I noticed the shine of the guy's shoes. He took a wide-brimmed hat from his head and placed it on the corner of the table. He had silver hair.

He shook my hand and introduced himself as Frank Boyd. He said, "I'd like to discuss the possibility that I might represent you, Mr Chase."

"I'm guessing you might be expensive, Mr Boyd."

"I am," he admitted. "Of course, if you'd prefer one of the court-appointed monkeys, that's certainly an option. They do find the legal system a bit of a challenge, but they're good with bananas."

"I don't have any money. My career has been on the slide for a while now. And I ... lost some." When Chloe ran off with it.

"I'm aware of that. In any case, the authorities have frozen all your funds pending trial." He opened his briefcase, took out a document and slid it across the desk towards me. "However," he said, and he looked like someone who had just laid down an excellent poker hand, "if you're willing to sign this then I'm willing to represent you."

"What is it?"

"It's a publishing contract. If you sign it you'll be giving us permission to publish all of your songs. Your previous publisher has agreed to release you from your existing contract. For a price, of course, but we're willing to cover that cost."

He took a pen from his pocket and passed it over to me.

"You really think I have a career after this?"

He smiled. "You're front page news, Mr Chase. I wouldn't be surprised if you're top of the charts this time next week, especially out in the far colonies. You're very popular out there, you know."

I glanced around the room. It was clean, tidy. It could have been anywhere, but my cell was no more than a hundred yards away. "You think they'll let me record my songs while I'm locked up here, Mr Boyd?"

"Let's not get ahead of ourselves," he said.

I started to read the contract but it was the usual legal-sleaze gobbledygook. The deal seemed good, and I obviously did not want to be represented by a court-appointed simian. So I signed.

He offered me a pack of cigarettes, which I accepted and I lit one up. Finally he got around to asking me: did I kill Johnny Tag? I told him I must have. He asked me why, and I told him I didn't know why. I didn't even remember picking up the knife.

Boyd promised to bring in some technical experts to see if there was any evidence of the Chloe mind-ware left in my head. I hadn't seen 'Chloe' since the stabbing but I figured there ought to be some trace of it. That gave me hope.

At the end of that first discussion, Boyd stood up and shook my hand. He put a business card on the table and pushed it across to me. Then he pressed his hat into place.

"Write some new songs, Mr Chase. We'll get you out of here, don't you worry. And just think of the publicity *that* will bring!"

The guard came to escort me back to my cell. I picked up Boyd's business card. It read:

GARR-DAVIS LEGAL SERVICES
Frank Boyd, Criminal Attorney
Representing clients from
the far colonies to the inner worlds

I said to the guard, "Is there a business card in my hand?" I held it up.

He looked confused but nodded his head. "Sure there is, Mr Chase. Sure there is."

I went back to the cell, sat on the bed and stared at the wall.

*

I went to court for a preliminary hearing. They had to take me in by some secret route because apparently I was attracting a lot of media attention. I had a pounding headache and felt sick as they led me into the courtroom. I looked up into the gallery and saw Jane Monet sitting there. I don't think I'd ever seen her outside The Golden Grill before. She looked very anxious. I sat down next to Boyd. After a few moments the judge asked Boyd to say his piece.

Boyd rose to his feet and straightened his jacket. "At this time we would ask that all charges against Raymond Chase be dismissed. There is clear evidence of memetic tampering in Mr Chase's mind."

The prosecutor immediately objected. "It is anything but clear that Mr Chase was coerced to attack the deceased, Jonathan Tag. It *is* clear that Mr Chase plunged a steak-knife into Mr Tag's chest and killed him."

The judge paused wearily, then surprised us all by saying, "I'd like to discuss this matter of 'Memetic Incursion' with the representative of the MPA before deciding whether to proceed. Is Miss Laine present?"

Laine? I started to turn around to look, and a dark-haired, slim young woman brushed past me to stand before the judge. I couldn't see her face at that moment but it was definitely Maia. *She* was the MPA expert for my trial? "Yes, your honour," she said.

"Then we will adjourn to my chambers," the judge declared. "Myself, Miss Laine, the Defendant, and counsel for defence and prosecution."

They led me away from the courtroom, which was buzzing with excited voices. I glanced up at Jane again and she managed a worried smile.

*

We all sat down. The room was very small, and I was disappointed there was no window. I wanted a view, something other than the walls of a cell or the interior of a courtroom.

"Memetic Incursion," the judge said. "Care to enlighten us, Miss Laine?"

"It's clear that you *do* need some help, your honour."

He raised an eyebrow.

"I mean the legal system," she clarified quickly, "it's not exactly geared up for this. Throughout the pre-trial statements, the term 'Memetic Incursion' is used incorrectly, in my opinion. It seems to have been assumed that the phrase refers to the viral mind-ware. The 'Chloe' software infection."

The judge shrugged. "Well, yes."

"Strictly speaking," Maia said, "a 'meme' is an idea — one that replicates. So 'Memetic Incursion' would mean: putting an *idea* into someone's head."

I didn't quite see what she was getting at.

"Yes, they uploaded some software into Mr Chase's mind," she continued, "but that was a means to an end. The important point to consider is why they did it. What did they hope to achieve? What idea did they mean to implant inside Mr Chase's head?"

The judge sat back in his chair. "Ah, I see. The idea was to kill Jonathan Tag."

"Exactly. Someone wanted to get rid of Johnny Tag. This was all about that."

I hadn't wanted to say anything because the conversation seemed to be going in my favour. But I found myself saying, "Chloe would never have..."

The judge held up a hand, cutting me off. He looked at Maia again. She said, "It may or may not have been Miss Hart. She might not be responsible for the avatar used to coerce Mr Chase. There certainly isn't enough evidence to convict her. Yet."

The judge shook his head. "We're in trouble. Our ability to judge innocence and guilt, so much depends on physical evidence. But it's getting harder and harder to tell who did what."

"I agree," Maia said, "but it would clearly be wrong for Raymond Chase to stand trial. He did nothing wrong. Maybe he was a bit quick to sign that publishing deal with Mr Boyd."

The judge stared at Boyd. "Yes, that was very opportunistic of you, Mr

Boyd."

Boyd shifted uncomfortably in his seat, but did not reply.

The judge said, "I'd like Counsel to step outside. I'd like a word with Mr Chase and Miss Laine only."

Both lawyers started to object, but then thought better of it and left.

The judge looked at Maia. "I understand you have a relationship with the Defendant."

"An ex-relationship, your honour, which we declared. I can bring in other colleagues from the MPA if you wish, but they will tell you the same as I have."

The judge stared into space for a long moment. "I have a feeling I'm going to have to throw this case out," he admitted at last. "I could do it right now, but I *am* going to talk to some of Miss Laine's colleagues, just to be absolutely sure."

I let go of a breath I didn't even know I was holding.

He said, "I have a feeling you're going to meet Chloe Hart again, Mr Chase. If she should admit to you that she is responsible for the death of Jonathan Tag, I want you to bring that information to Miss Laine, and I want her to bring that information to me. Do we understand each other?"

"Chloe never told me to kill him," I insisted.

Maia said, "Are you sure about that?"

I stared at her. I wasn't sure of anything.

"Oh come on, Ray," she snapped, sounding thoroughly exasperated. "You didn't buy all that crap about her being driven out of town by Tag, did you? Poor little Chloe, with one bag on her shoulder and her tail between her legs? Please!"

The judge said, "One thing I can tell you with certainty, Mr Chase, is that Chloe Hart currently works for Garr-Davis Publishing, as did Jonathan Tag. It doesn't quite fit with this idea that she ran away from him, now does it?"

I said, "If Chloe ever admits what she did, I'll bring it to Miss Laine."

A few days later I walked out of the courthouse a free man. The sun was blazing on the steps as I walked down to the street. I thought I saw Jane Monet in the crowd, looking at me and smiling. I would have gone to her but the reporters rushed in on me. Eventually Boyd came and helped me to get away, but by then I couldn't see any sign of Jane.

*

To cash in on the publicity, Garr-Davis Publishing set up a tour for me, across the chain of the outer colonies. The day I arrived for the first gig we were mobbed at the port. This apparently came as no surprise to the company, who had laid on more security than I'd ever imagined needing.

I'd learned that Chloe was high up in Garr-Davis, her position strengthened since the demise of Johnny Tag. I was hoping that when we reached the Caesar-5 colony I might get to see her. I was still playing 'Counting The Days' — a slightly sneering version — in hopes of annoying her. I sent a message saying I'd be in town, which went unanswered.

I'd heard Caesar had been beautifully terraformed, and it was true. For months, all I'd seen was jump gates, concert halls and the insides of hotel rooms. But I'd planned in having a couple of days off while on Caesar. No matter how famous you are, you can still move freely around a city if you dress convincingly like a regular person.

"Hey, you look just like Ray Chase," someone might say.

"Yeah, I get that a lot," I'd reply.

I had walked around the bay, admiring the sailboats, enjoying the laughter of families playing on the beach. I stopped for lunch at a small café, eating out on a balcony overlooking the water. You could smell the sea salt in the air and watch the local marine life at play — airfins leaping and eleseals warming their bellies in the sun.

I guess the security team were around somewhere, but they had orders to stay well back.

I looked up from my food and saw Chloe standing across the bench from me. "Hello, Ray," she said. She wore a chic business suit. It looked expensive, as did her hair. She had a diamond stud in her ear, which glistened brightly in the light reflecting off the water.

Despite myself, I found that I was smiling. "How'd you find me?"

She smiled too and sat down. "This whole tour was my idea," she said.

This was no great surprise to me. Frank Boyd had signed me to Garr-Davis Publishing, and the Caesar-5 branch was run by Chloe Hart. The job obviously suited her.

A waitress came to clear away my plate. Chloe asked for a bowl of chips and some mayonnaise. I ordered another beer.

"So how did you end up here?" I asked her. "What really happened when you left me, on Earth? I was … told … that you left to escape from Johnny Tag, but that can't be right."

She sighed. "I read all the transcripts from your court case, Ray. What the … avatar of me … told you, it was mostly right. I gave Tag the bootleg recordings, taken from my memories of you singing them to me. But Tag and I, we got on well. He didn't run me out of town; it was nothing like that. He set me up with this job and things have gone well for me."

"You look great," I said, and I meant it.

Her chips arrived and she began to eat them, two at a time and dipped in the mayo. For a moment she looked like the young girl I once knew.

"So you had nothing to do with what happened to me?"

The judge and Maia Laine, they wanted Chloe's confession, but I knew they weren't going to get it.

"Not until after," she said.

"After what?"

"Johnny's death. I heard about it almost immediately, through Garr-Davis channels. I heard you'd been arrested and I arranged for Frank Boyd to go see you. You obviously needed representation and I knew you didn't have any money. I wanted to get you under contract anyway, and I told Boyd to try to work that in."

I shook my head. "Slick,".

"The bootlegs do great business, Ray. Too good, in fact. You can get away with a little out here, but we take in a lot of money and we weren't paying back any royalties at all. Not to you anyway. That had to stop. Maybe Johnny's death was a message to tell us so, maybe it wasn't. In any case, getting you under contract was the right thing to do."

I nodded in a jaded kind of way. "I can't complain about the money," I said. "And it's nice to have bigger audiences. That's all any artist wants."

She looked at me sadly. Maybe she was questioning my use of the word 'artist'. Well I like to think I am one.

I said, "What I don't understand is the avatar itself. It seemed to be genuine. It knew things about us. The memories, they were real. They were changed, but they were real."

"I thought about that too," she said. "I thought about it a lot. Johnny Tag's spiders went through every corner of my mind, looking for songs you'd played to me. Maybe they took other stuff too. Memories of times we spent together. Enough information to build the avatar."

"But Tag wouldn't have been behind this."

"No. Johnny wasn't the suicidal type. No way did he set you up to kill him. But he did collect the data from me. I gave it up willingly. Maybe someone could have stolen it from him."

I sat back and tried to work that round in my mind. It was twisted but it made sense. So the question was, who had access to Tag's data, wanted him dead, and used me to get the job done? It still sounded like Chloe should be the main suspect, but I believed her when she said she had nothing to do with it.

She said, "You know there's no such thing as 'Garr-Davis Message Services' right? It sounds like one of our companies, but it isn't."

It figured.

"Let it go, Ray," she urged me. "Things turned out okay for you, didn't they?"

"Yeah," I said. "I guess things worked out better than okay."

She cleaned her fingers with a napkin. "I have to get going," she said. "Lots to do."

She came around to my side of the bench, sat down and hugged me for a moment. We smiled the way old friends do, knowing that we had grown very far apart but recognising our past together.

"I hear you still sing 'Counting The Days'," she said. "I like it, that you do."

Then she walked away and that was the last I saw of her.

*

After months of touring I made my way back to Earth. It's the nature of the business I'm in, to go away for months at a time, come back again and pick up where I left off. Have guitar, will travel. London was noisy and damp. As I walked down Oxford Street the rain fell in great sheets, so I dived into the first pub I came across. The place was empty, but there was an open fire near to the bar. I bought a pint and for a while I sat quietly, gazing into the flames. Then I called Maia Laine.

Maia was expecting me to contact her if I had evidence against Chloe, but I told her straight out that Chloe Hart was innocent.

"Then why are we here?" she asked. She looked pristine, like she was fresh out of a mould.

"I just wanted to thank you again," I said. "Without your testimony..."

She shrugged.

I said, "You and I, we ended on such bad terms when we split up."

"True," she replied, "but I knew you were a self-obsessed shit from the start. Anyway, it was just an adolescent infatuation. It doesn't matter now."

"Did we have a one-night stand, months before we started dating?"

"You finally remembered that, did you?" She smiled. "It was almost a year before. After a gig. You were off your head that night. Still grieving over Chloe, I expect."

I shook my head. I didn't want to rehash all of that again. I wanted to ask her about Tag. It still played on my mind. Someone had used me. Played me. It didn't sit well. "Did you have any other suspects?" I asked her. "Other than Chloe?"

"No."

"It had to be someone close to Tag," I said. "Someone who had access to the data plundered from Chloe's mind."

She frowned. "Things turned out the way they were supposed to, Ray. Tag was a thief. The MPA is delighted to see the back of him. It would have been nice to take out Chloe Hart too, but you can't win them all."

I stared at her. I hadn't expected her to be so callous.

"As for you, Ray," she went on, "well you're a big star now, as you always should have been. Be thankful."

It was only then that the nasty little thought occurred to me. I said, "I expect the MPA had been investigating Tag. Prior to his death."

She smiled. "Yes. We were trying to build a case against him. We knew how Tag was operating and we didn't like it."

"How did you know?"

"We worked undercover for months, inside his organisation. There was some evidence, but not enough to convict. It's becoming very difficult to prove anything against anybody."

"What kind of evidence? Chloe's memories?"

She leaned forward and looked at me closely. "If I were to admit that the MPA had access to Chloe's memories, that would make the MPA the prime suspect, wouldn't it? Obviously, I'm not going to do that."

My mood was turning very sour. "I almost went to jail."

She tilted her glass towards her and took a sip. "Now, Ray, there was never any chance of that. It was very clear that you were innocent."

"So everyone's happy."

"You're a success, Ray. And you're getting the proper reward for the music you create. That's what the MPA is here to safeguard. We're happy with the way things turned out. You should be too."

"I don't think I am," I muttered.

"Well that's a damn shame, Ray."

I sat back in my chair. She stood up and started to put her coat back on. She said, "I have to be somewhere."

"I guess so," I said, and drained my glass. "This undercover operation. How big was the MPA team?"

"We tend to work alone."

"That's what I figured."

"None of us are innocent in this business, Ray. Not even you. But you and I have one thing in common, at least. We're both trying to stay straight, and doing the best we can."

"I hope that's true," I said, and watched her leave.

I knew I didn't have enough to take to the judge. She hadn't actually admitted to anything, but I could read between the lines.

*

The doorbell jingle-jangled as I went inside. There were a couple of other customers in, but they were getting ready to leave. Jane looked at me as I sat down on a stool at the front counter. "It's me," I said.

"So it is. I heard you were in town." She still had beautiful skin, and she even had the smile. "Don't you have no place else to go?"

"You wait on tables, I sit on stools."

She laughed and asked me what I wanted to eat.

"I'd like the all-day breakfast, please."

She nodded, but didn't rush off to do anything. Behind the counter she had a beat up old radio, tuned to old time jazz. I said, "I was wondering if you would dance with me. I've wanted to, all this time."

She looked at me like she'd seen something move at the corner of her eye. "Ray Chase, I do believe that's the most straightforward thing you ever said to me."

This sounded vaguely promising so I stood up. I lifted up the hinged section of the counter and she came through. I held her close, and we danced right there among the tables while the music played.

"Your eyes are brown," I told her. "Did you know mine are blue?"

She rested her head against my shoulder. "Yes," she said. "I've known it for a long time."

Jane Monet. In that moment she was the chorus to my song. But deep down I know I can only come back to her so many times. People like me, we never settle down. Just have to keep moving on, to the next song and the next town.

Have guitar, will travel.

THE TIME TRAVELER'S SON

Jason Erik Lundberg

It was Wade's seventh birthday. There were presents and cake and ice cream in the backyard, and a colourful piñata shaped like a donkey, and twenty of Wade's friends from school. His mum had even hired a clown - a lazy clown, Wade could smell alcohol when the clown bent down and breathed, "Happy birthday." Crap at balloon animals, he was winded after blowing one up, and upon failing to twist or turn or knot it into a dog or giraffe or something, he would present the sausage of air and latex with a weak flourish, "It's a snake!"

Upstairs, in the house, Wade's dad finished packing. The lame clown forgotten and left to wheeze on a lawn chair and nip from a cheap silver flask, Wade asked his dad where he was going, why he wasn't down at the party.

"Important business, kiddo," said his dad. "Time travelling business. My first mission." He closed the suitcase and pointed out the window to the '84 Chevy Celebrity, bandage brown, rusted through, the fabric inside the roof coming unglued, hanging down, a drapery of obscuration.

"That's our car," Wade said.

"Oh no, kiddo, it's my time machine. I can chat with Marie Curie, or punch Hitler in the face, or have tea with an archaeopteryx. I can go anywhere I want, and any*when*."

"All your stuff is packed inside."

"It's a long trip. I may be gone for a while."

"But if it's a time machine, can't you return to right after when you left?"

Wade's dad ruffled his hair and smiled. "My son, the genius."

"So why was Mum yelling at you and calling you names?"

"Oh, that. She's ... just upset because I'm leaving, kiddo. She wants me to stay. But I can't. I've got some big responsibilities now, saving-the-world kind of responsibilities, and I don't want to shirk them."

"When will you be back?"

"Two weeks from today," said Wade's mum from the doorway, appearing from nowhere, a better trick than blowing up non-existent balloon animals. "Like it says in the custody agreement."

"Right, right." Wade's dad was distracted, lost in his thoughts. "Well, I suppose I'll be off then. Dinosaur hugs."

Wade gripped his dad's head and vice versa, and they clonked foreheads, both saying, "Clonk!" at the same time.

"Happy birthday, kiddo," said Wade's dad, and he grabbed his suitcase. Out the door, in the car, and it sputtered and farted blue smoke, and then it was around the corner and his dad was gone.

*

It was Wade's twenty-first birthday. He sat in a bar called the Café of the Asphyxiated Borough, a hole-in-the-wall near campus, decorated by a wood-cut of two disembodied hands strangling a donkey. He sat on a stool made of cracked leather and got legally drunk for the first time, with his father. Splitting a pitcher of watered-down lager, eating peanuts with way too much salt, they talked about Wade's future. A television bolted to the wall played a baseball game that everyone ignored.

"So you're really going to be a vet, huh?"

"Yeah," Wade said. "That's the goal. Graduate school first though."

"All kinds of animals, even the little ones?"

"Especially the little ones. Even hamsters. I don't want to be sticking my hands into cows and horses forever."

Wade's dad began to sing, "A horse is a horse, of course, of course..."

"Oh, Jesus."

"What?"

"You're doing it again."

Wade's dad smiled and signalled for another pitcher. "Yes, I always seem to be embarrassing you, don't I?"

"Not all the time," Wade said. "Just most of the time."

"Like the time I took you to the natural sciences museum and knocked over that display of stuffed birds?"

"Yeah. Like that."

"Or the time I was in the stands at your little league game and spilled beer all over my pants, so it looked like I peed in them?"

"You know, you really shouldn't have had beer at a children's baseball game in the first place."

"Or the time I took you to the steakhouse and you told me you were a vegetarian."

"I was a vegetarian. Am."

"You know, I was kind of hoping you'd go into the family business."

"Well, lawyering is all right for Mum, but it's not really my—"

31

"No, no, I wasn't talking about Mum."

"Oh, not this again."

"Come on! You'd get to see the world. Experience history for yourself, feel like you have purpose to your life."

"Dad, would you cut that shit out? I'm not seven any more. It's just a story. A dumb story."

Wade's dad looked into his beer. Wade had never seen him look so old, so worn down, as if he'd already lived several lifetimes, his hair a shocking white, the crow's feet and laugh lines etched into skin by chisel and time.

"Fine," his dad said. "Let's just drop it. Happy birthday, kiddo."

They finished the pitcher and then went their separate ways: Wade to his dorm room by campus bus, and his dad by cab to a roach-infested apartment downtown.

*

It was Wade's wedding day. He was marrying a pretty Chinese girl named Xiaxue. His mother had planned the event to perfection, driving him a bit crazy with it all actually, and his fiancée too, with the flowers and the catering and the venue and the band and the minister and the dress and the cake and all the minutiae. Wade and his fiancée wanted a small affair, but it ballooned from thirty people, to sixty, to a hundred fifty, to two hundred, and Wade didn't even care any more; he just wanted it all over with so he could start a life with his new bride. His mother, wanting to include Xiaxue's family in the celebration, since they were flying all the way from Hong Kong, had decorated the Wegener House with Chinese lanterns of red and gold, some labelled "love", some "happiness", some "prosperity". Also the flowers were all different vibrant colours, no white because white was a bad luck colour, and they were serving green tea and egg rolls alongside the numerous other heavy *hors d'oeuvres*. Xiaxue's family seemed pleased with the references to their culture.

The ceremony over, and Wade didn't trip over his shoes at all, and said all the right things in all the right places, and smiled a big smile after kissing his new bride on the lips, even slipping her a little tongue. They walked back into the house from the courtyard and prepared to meet and greet the two hundred guests. Dozens of "It's so good to see you", "Thank you for coming", "I'm glad you enjoyed the ceremony", "Yes, we got the fondue pot you sent", "I'm sorry, I don't know where the bathroom is" and "The food is right through there". There was hardly time to eat because everyone wanted to talk to him, or give him advice, or ask where they were going on the honeymoon (Greece). Relatives, friends or strangers continually put drinks in his hand, and the quantity of alcohol and lack of food were producing vertigo, a spinning room, a loss of equilibrium. So Wade didn't notice his father approach the table and start talking to his new wife.

"So you own a clinic?"

"Yes," she said, "Wade and I are going to run it together."

"You two met in veterinary school."

32

"That's right."

"Pets?"

"Mostly pets. Dogs, cats, hamsters. The occasional turtle or rabbit. We have an iguana in a terrarium in the waiting area who likes to sun himself all day under the heat lamp."

"You're from Hong Kong?"

"Yes," she said.

"So you know all about the exotic medical treatments over there?"

"Like?"

"Like dried oviduct fat of a Chinese forest frog for its curative powers," said Wade's dad.

He said, "Ground-up deer antlers or shark bone powder to boost vitality."

He said, "Desiccated tiger penis."

And without the slightest hesitation, she said, "Yes. I know about all of those."

"Have you ever used any of them?"

"No. My grandparents will sometimes use the frog, but that's about it. And since deciding to become a vet, it's hard for me to use any animal products now. The closest would be tiger balm for sore muscles, but that's not made from tigers."

"Tiger *blam,*" Wade said, and the husband and wife smiled at a shared joke.

"It looks like you've picked a winner, kiddo," proclaimed Wade's dad. "You make sure to hang on to this one."

Wade smiled, lightheaded, and burst out laughing.

"You know what story this man used to tell me when I was a kid?" he slurred.

"Wade," said his dad, "I don't think this is the time—"

"He said he was a *time traveller!*"

"Wade," said his new wife, "honey, are you feeling all right?"

"A *time traveller!* Can you believe that? He didn't want to admit to being a bad husband and a bad father and so he made up this story about trekking up and down the space-time continuum, making himself all important and not accepting any responsibility for … hey let go o' me!"

Wade jerked his arm away and the contents of his champagne glass splashed over the front of his father's ill-fitting and flyblown suit. Hushes from the crowd. The band even stopped playing "Night Train" in mid-bar.

Wade's father looked down at the slowly spreading stain and said, "Maybe I shouldn't have come."

Wade sat down, not quite sure what had just happened.

"I'll leave," said Wade's dad.

"No, please," Xiaxue entreated him. "Please don't go. We'll get some club soda for it."

"No, no, this was a mistake." He turned. "Congratulations, son," he said, and left.

*

It was Wade's dad's last day alive. The hospital stank of industrial cleanser and urine and death. The terminal ward, where his dad was kept, was a fog of depression, the air itself bringing you down. All around were the sniffles or muffled cries of the soon-to-be survivors, those left behind when loved ones passed on.

Every so often a doctor or nurse would come in, check the chart, inspect the beeping machines, do something with the I.V. Wade saw a detachment in their eyes, a coldness, a defence mechanism for the pervading climate of death they had to face every day. The candy stripers were the only perky visitors, though they had nothing of substance to say.

Diagnosis: a worn-out heart. The doctors couldn't figure it out. "It's like his organs are twice as old as they should be," they said. "He's sixty-two, but his heart shows the strain of a centenarian."

Jet-lagged from the twenty-five hour flight from Hong Kong, Wade barely noticed when his father awoke from a deep sleep.

"Kiddo?"

"Yeah, it's me."

"When'd you get here?"

"About an hour ago. Right from the airport."

"Where's your lovely wife?"

"The doctors said she shouldn't fly at eight months. It could hurt the baby."

"Right, right."

"She wanted to be here."

A weak smile. "I bet she did. Give her a kiss from me when you get back."

"I will."

"Sorry I won't be around to see that new baby of yours."

"Dad, don't talk like that."

"But it's true. I'll be surprised if I last the day."

"Dad..."

"What do you think happens?" his dad said. "You know, when we go?"

"I don't know."

"I read up a lot on the afterlife, even talked to some theologians and philosophers in my travels. No one seems to agree.

"There's the Christian Heaven, or Hell, where either you have paradise and get to see your family again, or little men in red pyjamas poke you with pitchforks. But then I think, what if I get to Heaven and my really annoying relatives are there and they won't leave me alone, and I can't go anywhere else because, well, it's Heaven. I'd almost prefer pitchforks to that.

"There could be Buddhist reincarnation, which I like a lot. They don't see people as having souls, but more of a collection of sensory inputs, and that you never truly die but change from one form to another. Just like you're not the same person as you are when you're six years old as you are when you're sixty, it's the same with becoming a new person. We are reborn every day, if you think like this, with your cells constantly dying and being replaced; every seven years you're a whole new person, and so it's not much of a leap. Your karma determines your new body. With my luck I'd probably become a snail.

"Or there could be nothingness, annihilation, the void of emptiness. All your experiences, all your memories, gone, poof, just like that. Your body returned to the earth to feed the worms and enrich the soil, but your soul, your identity, is just gone, lost forever."

Wade started to cry, unable to hold it in, the exhaustion and the sadness of this place and the discussion of the afterlife just too much. He covered his face with his hands. He thought of the helpless ignorance of what lay beyond, that undiscovered country, that awfully big adventure. He rested his head on the bed and his father patted his head.

"Shush now, don't be sad. If I come back as a snail, I'll visit you every day."

"I'm sorry I called you a bad father."

"Oh don't worry about that. I wasn't the best father, though I tried."

"I know you did."

"Besides, I've seen you, with your family, years from now. You speak Cantonese and your son grows up into a handsome man, a book publisher, and he visits every other weekend with his girlfriend, who becomes his wife, a beautiful woman, who looks like she should model lingerie but she's a physicist. You and your wife grow happy and content, running the animal hospital even into your old age, revered by your community as the vets who are truly there for their patients. Your grandson, the piano prodigy, he has his father's eyes, your eyes, my eyes, the eyes of every male in our family line. It's the eyes, Wade, the eyes, the eyes..."

His father's words drifted away as if caught on a breeze, and his chest raised and lowered several more times and then went still. Wade's cheeks and ears burned, hot enough to steam the air. The room, the ward, became instantly quiet. No squeak of shoes, no hiss from ventilators, no hum of life-monitoring electronics. No inhale of breath. The clock on the wall, analogue, ancient, spaded hands wrought of centuries-old iron, still, unmoving, halted. To tick no more.

Time stopped.

DOLLS

Colin P. Davis

Mandi's difficulties with the doll started shortly after her pseudo-mother was arrested by Robot Rentals. The two women who arrived to do the job wore pinstripe suits and an air of aloofness. By the time they finally frog-marched their captive down the path to the waiting cart, both engineers were unkempt and red-cheeked with embarrassment — and Mandi was giggling uncontrollably.

Her mother's cries were too much for Dad. He grabbed one of the women by the sleeve. She impaled him with a stare.

"Don't kill her," he said.

Mandi stood at the door with her doll in hand. She watched the suddenly frozen scene in fascination. Four grown-ups, for once with no words to say. Nothing moved except the slow clouds of breath from the three humans; her mother had never breathed.

Then the engineer shook Dad free. She gave him an almost-smile. "It's not like she's got feelings...."

Mandi shuddered in the icy air as an icier satisfaction suffused her body. She let the lady doll slide from her fingers. As always, it landed on its feet. It straightened up, head at Mandi's knee height. *No … large or small, dolls don't have feelings.* But humans do, and Mandi had been pushed too far. She couldn't exactly put a name on the emotion, but she'd known how to make it go away.

That evening, Dad tried his best to maintain a willow-flexible demeanour; *que sera sera.* However, his short fuse and chain-drinking were clear evidence to Mandi that he did not relish spending the night without his soft, cyber-companion. Mandi suspected she should feel guilty. It amused her that she did not.

After dinner, she spent an hour sweating in the multi-gym, another hour in the aromatherapy suite, then retired to the virtual booth to wrestle Martians, until eventually the doll chased her upstairs to her bedroom.

*

"I'm going to kill you, Em," Mandi growled through clenched teeth. Her face folded in petulant ugliness. "If you don't shut up about Mother, I swear I'm going to kill you." The old bed grumbled and groaned as Mandi, pudgy and pink-pyjamaed, bounced up and down on the mattress. The moulded frame — formed in the shape of a laurel leaf — squeaked against the concrete floor. The water-jug rattled.

The doll smiled placidly. "Mother knows best, Miss Mandi. And don't do that! Mother's told you not to do that. What if you fall?"

With patience, the thin whine of words could be deciphered, and Mandi and her father had no problem. Her pseudo-mother had insisted the doll spoke gibberish; Mandi found that funny, particularly as the doll had been programmed for unquestioning maternal support.

"But Mother's not here," Mandi pointed out, twisting her face into one of her best sneers. She lay back on the bed and held the doll above her face, so close she could smell its acrid scent. "You may recall she was carted off just after lunch." Mandi pressed her forefinger into the doll's sharp and rigid nose. "I know you remember everything."

"I'm sure she had a reason for popping out," the doll said.

"Popping out!" Mandi yelled. "Her heels ploughed furrows in the gravel. Anyway … she's not my mother. My real mother ran away with a Doc Savage doppelgänger."

The doll shook its head, emulating disapproval. "You're far too disrespectful for a little girl."

"I'm *not* a little girl! I only *look* eight!" Mandi squeezed the small, hard body until she imagined that, like a nut-shell, it would crack apart under the pressure. "Don't underestimate me."

The doll struggled to be released. "Put me down, Miss Mandi! Put me down!"

But Mandi merely giggled, enjoying the fraudulent cruelty.

"And another thing, Em…." She shook the screeching toy, laughing as its head wobbled limply, then tossed it onto the bed. "I'm not doing the competition tomorrow. I've had enough dressing up. I've had enough pretending."

The doll twisted into a sitting position and, with sharp, precise motions of its tiny pink hands, tried to regain its dignity. Tight blonde curls were brushed, the blue dress smoothed out. Finally the toy whined, "Your father would be furious. He stands a good chance of winning this time. Lucy Aimes's run of luck can't last forever."

"No, it's *me* that stands a good chance of winning! Me! Not him! Since when did my dad dress up? Did he ever perform, apart from Scrooge?" Mandi placed her bare sole over the doll and forced it down into the mattress. It continued to talk. The vibrations tickled her. She bounced from the bed.

"…and he's put so much money into your training and your wardrobe. You

37

should be more grateful."

Mandi swung around and glared at the doll. "I want to be allowed to grow up. I'd be grateful for that."

She strode purposefully to the door and grabbed the imitation hardwood handle, but she did not turn it. She was not allowed out of her room this late, and certainly not with the doll watching, ready to tell; luckily, the doll was not quite as smart as its designer dress.

"I'm hungry," Mandi said. "Dad's forgotten that Mother always brings my supper up by nine." Perhaps she'd been a bit hasty in arranging for Mother's demise. She hadn't thought ahead to suppertime.

"Mother knows best," the doll insisted. Mandi imagined its rigid smile twitched upwards at the sides.

She rushed to the bed and smothered the smiling — *always smiling!* — face with her sweaty palm. The doll struggled. Giggling, Mandi dropped the doll head-first into the empty water-jug, where it prattled away hollowly. Its elegant black dress shoes, which stuck inelegantly out of the top, kicked about, then gave up.

Mandi clambered onto the bed and began to trampoline again.

In the oak-leaf mirror — propped lopsidedly on the rickety and ancient dressing table as if freshly fallen from some great glass tree — another girl bounced. Fine, feathery black hair flowed about her face, drifting smoothly, as though beyond the glass the clear syrup of time flowed at an easier pace. She knew the visual delay was not an illusion, but an aspect of the mirror's interactive circuitry — should a spot dare to appear on her perfect skin, the mirror would ring it with a glowing green circle — but it still made her feel unreal, as though she were living a fairy tale.

She was disgusted by her prettiness. If she'd been a really ugly, warty, pock-marked hog of a child, she would not have had to compete in these ridiculous pageants for the last fifteen years.

She leapt down to the worn pink carpet and swept her arm over the dressing-table, scattering cosmetics and her teddy bear collection from the top. Then, running her finger through the dust on the mirror, she traced the outline of her face and added spots and a huge nose. But what would she really look like if she was ever allowed to grow up? What would it be like to have breasts, and long elegant legs? What would her dad think of that! And would she think differently herself, being older, and without the drugs? How could she know? She was trapped in this infant mind.

Tears blurred the image in the mirror.

She guessed her true age was twenty-one, maybe twenty-two. "How many years have been stolen from me?" She often spoke to her reflection; apart from the irritating doll it was her only companion. Her father would allow no visitors and she was too old for school. Of course, she knew it couldn't answer — she wasn't a child!

With her sleeve she dabbed at her eyes.

She sat a while and gazed at the frost on the window. It was dark outside, apart from the headlamps of the occasional trawler, cruising the streets for free-dolls careless enough to make themselves conspicuous.

Of course, Em was right. Mandi did stand a chance of winning this year. She'd earned a good sum as runner-up in the regional pageants and her Helen of Troy at Birmingham had lifted her into the favourites. In truth, she knew she was way out in front — the only usurper capable of dethroning Queen Lucy.

Mandi took the doll's legs, pulled it from the jug, and dropped it on the bed. Immediately it sat up, hands clasped to its temples, as if it had a headache.

"You've been told not to do that, Miss Mandi!" The voice was incapable of harshness, but the electronic whine somehow achieved a sharper edge. "Time and time again. Why must you be so disobedient?"

Mandi shoved it from the bed, but the doll was quick and grabbed at her pyjamas, dragging the pink sleeve down over her hand. She flung the doll back and forth, but it hung on. She tore it free and tossed it across the room. The doll flipped like a cat and landed on its feet. Mandi snatched up a pillow and hurled it. She missed.

The doll stood, hands on hips. "Well if you've worked all that out of your system now, perhaps we could actually *communicate.*"

"Okay," said Mandi. She relaxed her shoulders and eased her breathing, then pulled back her elongated sleeve. "Em... I'm hungry. Get me some food!"

*

The next day was Saturday — a day normally reserved for shopping with Dad. They could spend half the day beachcombing around second-hand stores and flea markets, rooting out bargain medicines, cheap cosmetics and period clothes. Mandi enjoyed shopping. Occasionally, they would stumble across a neat little robot aid, or some other mechanical curiosity. That was how they had found Em, the doll. At the time, it had seemed like a good find.

This Saturday, however, Dad was off to the Pavilion to make final arrangements for Sunday's Championship Pageant, and Mandi had to get to the switch-doctor to settle her debt. Arranging for Mother's breakdown had been expensive. Luckily, she knew where Dad hid the prize money she had earned over the years. Dolls were intelligent, but not very wise; Em, in particular, managed to combine a nice line in clever-sounding statements with a moronic simple-mindedness that at times had Mandi screaming, *"You're just not paying attention!"* So it had been child's play to mislead Em into revealing the location of Dad's midnight scrooge-fests. He was a *cash only* man and had to stash it somewhere. Did he really imagine that if he counted it often enough, the cash might multiply?

It would be only a matter of days now before he needed to examine the notes again and discovered the shortfall. He would be furious with her. But he wouldn't touch her; she was too valuable. There would be no chocolate for a few weeks, but she could face that. She'd got what she wanted.

She'd got rid of another whore.

*

Mandi closed the front door and surveyed the sunlit garden. Morning frost lay on hedges, lawn and trash. She gazed through the mist of her own breath at the doll, which walked up the gravel path ahead of her. Mandi wanted it to fall on its face, but she knew the doll would disappoint her. She followed. At the gate, the doll waited.

The gate was white with ice. Mandi opened it carefully with a pink-gloved fingertip. It wasn't that she was overly dainty, but the wood was so rotten Mandi suspected it was only the ice holding it together. Come spring there would be merely a scattering of sawdust on the path and nothing to keep out the puppy-dolls and vagrant animatrons.

This was typical of Dad — if he would not spend a few dollars on a gate, he was never going to spend serious money on her costumes. Everything she owned was cheap or second-hand, even this warm pink coat which he had swindled off the back of a Rentakid doll suffering a defective generosity impulse.

"Enlighten me, Em," Mandi said, as she shuffled along the sidewalk in her heavy boots. A backbone of leafless dead elms stretched down the central island of the boulevard. "Why do I give a damn about who sleeps with my father?" She skipped to catch up with the doll, leaping over a small green snake which slithered across her path on its multiple miniature wheels.

"Asking me that question, Miss Mandi, would suggest you've forgotten I'm just a toy." The doll did not break its stride or look back at Mandi.

On a stone gatepost a mechanical robin sang, twitching its head to watch Mandi as she passed.

"Sometimes I can't believe you're just a doll, Em."

"Sometimes I can't believe you're just a little girl."

"I keep telling you ... I'm *not* a little girl!"

Then Mandi laughed. The doll was winding her up — that was it. She folded her arms tightly. It must have been at least five below. She hated these long winters. "I'd like to meet your designer one day ... and poke her in the eye."

Mandi glanced over to the centre of the boulevard. On the grass lay the body of a man, his clothing frosty-white and scruffy. No doubt another doll, drained and lifeless. You could see them everywhere. Nobody bothered with bodies any more.

A pizza van purred swiftly towards them and in its wake came a horde of yapping puppy-dolls — growth-arrested strays; toys of flesh and blood, as much dolls as any animatronic construct. When they spotted Mandi, the dogs abandoned their attempt to catch the van and bounded towards her. Mandi had to stop as the animals threatened to trip her up. She recognized these as Labrador pups, and all colours: black, tan, white, green....

They were harmless, but a nuisance. They nuzzled at the doll, panting, sniffing, growling. The noise was so intense, and so funny, that Mandi did not become aware of the whirring of the approaching balloon until it was almost too late.

She recognized the familiar propeller sound of the toy Zeppelin at the same moment that a shadow fell upon the brick wall to her right. Years of suspicion and distrust had given her lightning reactions to the unexpected. She fell to the side. Puppies scattered. She bounced on one hip and rolled onto her knees, glancing up as she came to a halt against the wall.

Only meters away, the small helium-filled toy hovered. A fine spray was falling through the air below it, precisely where Mandi had been. The puppies began to yelp and snap at the air, turning in rapid, distressing circles. Then they dashed off, tumbling over each other in their panic.

Some type of chemical, maybe acid, Mandi realized — and intended for her.

The motor whine rose in pitch as the airship turned, bringing its camera around to target on Mandi.

"Em! It's after me!"

The doll had been outside the danger area and now ran towards Mandi.

The airship began to close the distance.

Mandi sprang to her feet, scooped up the doll and ran. A moment later she reached a gap in the wall and turned down the path to the canal.

"It's trying to burn me, Em," Mandi gasped as she ran. She held the doll in front of her face. "It wants to scar me."

"That would seem unlikely, Miss Mandi. What would be the purpose in disfiguring you?"

Mandi rapped the doll on the head with her knuckles. "The pageant of course! Someone wants to win … really badly."

The path zigzagged down the hill towards the canal. The airship, following a straight line, was gaining on her.

Mandi glanced backwards and slipped on the icy surface. She stumbled into a faster run, but kept on her feet. She leapt down a flight of brick steps to the towpath and hurried along the edge of the frozen waterway.

The Zeppelin was only a short distance behind. The whirring sound grew louder as they moved between the towering walls of the warehouses. Mandi's footsteps echoed as her heavy boots slapped against the cobbles. She followed the canal as it swept around a corner. Then she came upon a tall mesh fence. It stretched completely across the canal; the buildings ahead were to be demolished. Mandi could go no further.

She turned, went to run back, halted, hesitated... Her legs were trembling. She could see the gondola clearly now, a grey box hung on wires below the balloon. The box had three propellers and a central eye which must have been the camera. The propellers slowed.

No time to weigh the dangers; the ice seemed her only choice. If she could just outflank the airship, move faster and get behind. Grasping the mesh fence with her one free hand, she placed a foot upon the frozen canal, then transferred her weight. The ice creaked and cracked. Her boot vanished up to the ankle. She yanked it out, sending chunks of ice skidding across the frozen canal. Her grip on the fence held, but her arm was shaking.

She held the doll up. "I'm trapped, Em. I can't escape."

The airship was too close. She expected the acid spray to come at any moment. But the remote pilot must have known Mandi was trapped and was not going to waste a hasty shot.

"Spread your weight, Miss Mandi."

She had no other option. She released the fence and, in a swift, fluid motion, swam forward on the surface of the canal. The ice held. She tried to wriggle away, one hand dragging on the ice, the other still gripping the doll. But the airship turned again to cut her off. She began to cry. She couldn't believe this was happening. Would they really try to burn her, to destroy her prettiness? If only she was as agile as the doll....

"Em...." Mandi held the doll up.

"Yes, Miss Mandi?"

"Hold on tight!"

She hurled the doll towards the airship. Time seemed to slow as the toy floated up — like watching it happen in her mirror. The doll struck the balloon and, with its arm, hooked one of the suspension wires. The airship turned with the impact and pitched under the doll's weight. Then it began to sink. A cloud emerged from the gondola as the acid sprayed out away from Mandi, but covering the doll. The descent to the ice was swift. The doll's feet touched down first and then everything halted. The airship would not fall further; neither could it rise.

The remote pilot released the acid again, but the doll held on.

The propellers protested.

Mandi crawled to the rear, blindside of the camera. "Are you all right, Em?"

The doll did not answer.

Mandi closed in from behind, grabbed a sharp chunk of ice, which she had earlier kicked loose, and struck the airship as hard as she could manage. The balloon popped and deflated and fell. Useless propellers beat against the ice, then stopped.

"Em?"

The doll freed itself from the wires and limp fabric and stumbled from the wreckage.

"Well done, Em." Mandi smiled. "But your dress is ruined."

"I'll take your word for that."

Mandi giggled, though she felt no amusement. "I thought you had a sharp sense of style. Don't you recognize a rag when you see it?"

"Miss Mandi.... I appear to be blind."

*

"What were you doing this morning, going to the switch-doctor?"

It took immense control for Mandi to smother her surprise at the question. She scooped up another spoonful of beans and shovelled it into her mouth. Then she looked across the ranks of sauce bottles at her father. "Who says I went there? Have you got spies now?"

"Why else would you be down by the canal?"

Dad was right. There was no other reason. "I thought he might be able to fit Em with an off switch — she's been getting on my nerves. But that was before the attack. Now we need new eyes at the least, and she'll never look pretty again."

"You've no money."

"But *you* have."

Her father grunted and returned to eating his beans.

In truth, she'd only asked the switch-doctor, or Vance as he preferred, to clean up the doll. Then, no sooner had she paid her debt, he'd tempted her with another offer. A drug this time. *The* drug. The most important drug in the world to her. One dose would restore her body to natural ageing and neutralize the youth drugs permanently. She had to have it. But the price he wanted....

What was left of her winnings would not cover it, and even if it had, her father would never pay. He was the one keeping her in this condition. She should have hated him for that, and at times she did. But somehow it never lasted.

She watched him now as he ate. His eyes were on the slim waitress who was clearing the tables. He was a thin-faced man, not traditionally attractive, certainly not in this age of designer faces. His nose was short for a man and his skin was blemished by a youth of chemical abuse. But she admired him. He'd had the money, from her winnings, to change himself. The world was full of Bradley Pitts, Steve McQueens and Doc Savages. It took strength of character — or poverty — to stay true to the face and body you were born with.

And another thing.... He was still here to take care of her, while she didn't have a clue where her mother was.

Mandi finished off the last of the bland beans. "Are you going to ask her out?" she said.

He was startled for a moment. "What? Oh her? She's a doll."

Mandi knew he was guessing. The differences between automatons and humans were subtle, particularly with enhanced humans. Both appeared to be perfect.

"That's never stopped you before," she said, regretting the words almost as they set out from her lips.

"Are you finished?" he snapped. "I want to get to the bottom of this attack. If you're right and Lucy Aimes is involved, I'll break her mother's legs."

And he would. Mandi placed her spoon into the empty bowl and sat back. She smiled. Yes, he certainly would.

*

Mandi had to get that drug. She needed cash. Or she had to find something valuable to barter. It would probably be worth another visit to the switch-doctor. At the very worst, she could try crying.

Two hours before sunset, doll in hand, she set out again across the sunlit streets to Vance's basement workshop. The place had been a burger bar in the better days before the animatron glut and market crash, and a faded menu in the window still promised *Real Vegetables*.

Mandi ran down the stairs and pushed open the glass door. A bell rang.

43

The shop was dark and cold; Vance would be working in the back. After a moment, Mandi could make out a strange apparatus in the centre of the room. It reminded her of a dentist's chair. That had not been there in the morning. Vance was always up to something new.

"I wish you could see this, Em."

A door opened. A man appeared silhouetted in the rectangle of light. "I knew you'd be back," he said. She couldn't make out his face, but the corona of his shining skull was unmistakably Vance.

"That's not so smart. You know what I want."

He laughed and came forward. "You've got quite a mouth on you for one so … apparently young."

"I can't get enough money. I told you that before." Mandi held up the doll. "I can't even afford to get Em's eyes replaced. I was thinking maybe I could do some work for you."

Vance waved his hand and the ceiling illuminated. On a high shelf a row of Pierrot dolls turned their heads to face him.

"I don't need help," he said. "Business is just fine. In fact, I'm branching into new areas."

Mandi examined his face — though it was too good-looking to be his own face. What had he looked like as a child, before growing the movie star looks?

"This place could do with a dusting." Mandi ran her finger over the work table beside the dentist's chair. There was no dust at all.

"To pay for that drug you'd be dusting for the next fifteen years."

"In fifteen years I'll still be this little girl height, still have this little girl face, and still have the same little girl voice … if I don't get it."

"You could run away from home — go cold turkey."

"How would I live? I'm not rich, or did you miss that bit?"

"Or get *rescued* by one of those activist groups."

"Did you hear what they did to that girl's father in Seattle?" Mandi screwed up her face. "I don't hate my dad that much."

"Then there's the business I'm moving into. Not strictly ethical, but who cares about that these days?" He crossed to the dentist's chair. "This cost me an arm and a leg. There's a huge growing market in mind porn. Do you know what that means?"

"I'm not a child. You know that." But she had no idea what it meant.

"So you'll understand how much money is involved. It's staggering what some people will pay to have their mind abused by someone else's emotions."

"And what's the point you're presumably getting to?"

"Your mind could pay for your drug."

"Me…? What am I worth? I haven't lived yet. My body hasn't even been allowed to reach puberty. I know that. I've read about it."

"You'd be surprised what interests some people."

"Like my feelings and emotions? I'm good at getting mad at my father…. Would anyone pay for that?"

He studied the chair, lifted a head-sized hemisphere of gold mesh from behind it. "Oh yes."

"What do you think, Em?" Mandi lifted the doll close to her face. The charred cheeks and white eyes were an upsetting sight. "Tell me."

"Why ask a doll?" wondered Vance.

"Miss Mandi values my judgement." The doll turned its unseeing eyes towards Vance. "You have difficulty with duplicity, Miss Mandi. You have yet to learn that grown-ups have two faces."

Vance curled his top lip. "The doll doesn't really know you, does it? Anyway, the psychoanalysis is a bit rich, coming from something that only mimics life — an artificial being."

"It seems to me that we're all artificial to some extent," said Mandi. "You, me and Em. We're all dolls."

She liked that. It sounded clever. But that did not mean that she'd understood what Em had said. Sometimes she had to agree that the doll spoke gibberish. That designer had earned another poke in the eye.

Vance hefted the hemisphere in his hand. "With this machine I can record your emotions. It's called Amigdalation. Looks like nothing, but it's going to be massive."

Mandi sucked in her cheeks and pouted her lips, aware that she must have looked like a fish. She started to giggle.

"Is it a deal?" he asked.

Mandi groaned. "Seems a bit sick."

"People are complex." Vance stroked her hair; she drew back. "You're very sweet," he said.

The doll at Mandi's side spoke: "Sweetness is a concept put about by sour people."

Vance ignored the doll. "You fascinate me, Mandi. I can't even begin to imagine the contradictory emotions you must experience. The questing for self-image, the confusion of sexuality. Pushed forward into womanhood, dragged back into childhood...."

"You're quite verbose for a chipmonkey," said the doll.

Mandi lifted it to her face. "Em.... Shut up!"

Vance laughed. "I like you, Mandi. Tell you what.... I'll throw in new eyes for the doll too. Is it a deal?"

Mandi climbed up into the chair and took the mesh helmet from him. She put it over her head. There was room to spare.

"Just make sure I'm home before sunset."

*

Lying on her bed that evening, Mandi was confused and concerned. She didn't understand what Vance had done. It had seemed simple, but she suspected she was missing something.

He had made pictures form in her mind. At first she'd thought she was seeing them, but they were still there with her eyes shut. There were images of happy children and tragic children; youngsters using recreational drugs and music idols indulging in simulated intimacy. There were images of young women in various stages of growing up, and there were pictures of her father — so many pictures of her father that she'd become uncomfortable in a way she could not explain. And the young women had made her more aware than ever of the deficiencies in her own body, the changes that were forever postponed.

But she had the drug now! The doll had protested and advised her not to use it. But Mandi didn't care. She couldn't see why the doll was complaining — Em had new eyes, if not a new dress. They'd both done all right out of the switch-doctor.

She had considered taking the drug immediately, but there were so many things to weigh up first. Her life would change totally and forever. She had to prepare herself. Her father would possibly never forgive her.

Her sleep that night was fitful and punctuated by nightmares in which her body was bleeding from eyes and nose and navel. Her naked legs were slick and red. She awoke sweating to the cold light of the dawn sky. It was a welcome distraction to sit at the dressing-table and begin to prepare herself for the pageant.

*

The audience was huge; the pre-curtain noise intense. *Young At Heart* danced from the PA system. The excitement was like an energy source, powering Mandi into a state of high motivation. She had not taken the drug, not yet, but she had the tiny bottle with her. It would be excellent, she thought, to take it just before the contest started and to know this would be her last time at this event. The effect would not be evident immediately, except in her smug smile.

"Twenty minutes," a voice declared outside her dressing room. She heard the repeating words trailing away past the other rooms. Her father closed the door, then helped her slip into her Chinese Princess costume.

It would not matter now if Lucy Aimes won again, which she almost certainly would, for the fifth year running. Next year Lucy would again be an eight-year-old child on the pageant circuit, but Mandi would finally be one year older. Winning didn't really matter that much any more.

However, it mattered very much to her father. He would be disappointed to lose again, and devastated when she had to reveal her treachery.

Mandi looked at the doll, which was sitting on the table and leaning back on the light-ringed mirror. Just above its head she saw her father's reflection gazing at her.

"Why so serious, Mandi?" he said. "You can only do your best."

She would not feel guilty! This was her life. It was time to move on and grow up, time to show her father what she could be … the woman she was meant to be.

"I have a good feeling about this year's competition," he said. He waved a hair brush in his hand. "I couldn't find out who was behind the attack, but if Lucy was involved she'd know we would suspect her." He began to tidy Mandi's hair, but she snatched the brush from him. He could never get it right. "That should put her on edge," he said.

"What's her Original this time?" Mandi asked.

"The program says her mother has put words to Vivaldi's *Winter*."

"I hope Lucy gets frostbite."

Five minutes later Mandi was on stage, behind the curtain, with all the other girls and their retinue. As was customary, she encountered a degree of lightweight jostling as she threaded in and out of the tall cardboard trees in front of the dark-forest backdrop. There were a couple of new faces here; perhaps first-timers, genuine eight-year-olds. Every pageant she saw a few new kids. One year, someone had even tried to pass off a doll, but it had been picked up by the age test.

All the girls' costumes were extravagant, jewel-studded fountains of fabric. There was so much gold and glitter under the lights that at times the scintillating reflections dazzled Mandi. She found herself sniggering. *Like fairies at a stardust convention,* she thought. It was good that she could laugh at all this — she was already distancing herself from show-business.

She climbed onto a plastic rock and looked about for her father. He was over the far side of the stage, chatting to an attractive young woman. They were laughing. Mandi could always tell when he was flirting. She felt inside her costume to the comforting smoothness of the drug bottle. Time to take it; she'd hesitated too long. She jumped down and crossed the stage to where she'd tossed the doll up into a fake nest in a cardboard tree.

She attempted a loud whisper, trying to overcome the noise of the impatient audience hidden beyond the curtain and the more subdued conversation on the stage: "Are you all right, Em?"

The doll peeked over the side of the nest. "I know you still have the drug, Miss Mandi. I hope you will be sensible and not use it."

"Why should I listen to you? Why should I listen to anyone?"

"Mother knows best."

"Mother? What mother?"

"From my vantage point I can see your father. It seems you may have another mother before too long."

"Not if I have anything to do with it."

"Talking to yourself, Mandi?" Lucy Aimes appeared beside her. Even Mandi had to admit that Lucy's snowflake costume was superb. And her blonde curls....

"Those aren't real," said Mandi, as she tugged gently at the waist-length tresses.

"If I stuck to real, I'd be stuck with hair like yours."

"Does that go for your nose too?"

Lucy sneered, which involved squashing her nose until she resembled a piglet, then laughed. "So you're performing a Tai Chi ballet. Sounds a bit silly to me."

"You must be disappointed I'm actually here, after the balloon stunt."

Lucy's brow pinched tight and her eyes squinted. Mandi realized her rival knew nothing about the attack. That quizzical look could not be faked.

"I hope you fall over," said Lucy.

Just then large hands grabbed Lucy's shoulders and turned her away. Lucy's mother leaned in, face to face with Mandi. "Don't you upset my Lucy, you little monster." Her voice was quiet and tobacco flavoured. "Don't imagine you'll ever beat Lucy. They shouldn't even allow low-status trash like your father to enter these pageants."

At first Mandi was scared, but then her anger grew and she stood as tall as she could manage and glared at the beautiful white-haired witch. "You don't frighten me."

"Well what does frighten you? Losing your looks? Drowning under ice?" She smiled, revealing yellowed teeth. Now Mandi knew who had arranged the attack on her.

"This is a pageant," said Mandi. "Not a war."

"We'll see."

"Last refreshments, girls." A steward appeared with a tray of plastic cups.

Lucy's mother slipped away into the crowd.

Lucy appeared again and took a cup of orange juice from the tray. Mandi did the same, then moved over to the tree where the doll was perched.

Facing the tree and hunching her shoulders for privacy, she pulled the drug bottle out of her dress. It was time.

Lucy was behind her. "I don't know why you bother turning up at every pageant. You know you're second-rate. And you can only afford third-rate costumes. I'll be winning for the next ten years … or as long as I want."

"So what? It doesn't matter." Mandi kept facing the tree. She had the bottle in one hand and her cup of orange in the other. With her thumb, she flipped the bottle lid open. If only Lucy would move away.

"So what? Winning is everything," said Lucy from behind her. "You're either a winner or a loser. My mum says you're a loser. And I'm a winner." Even over the noise of the audience, Mandi could hear Lucy sipping her drink.

"And your mother is always right…" Mandi remarked dryly.

"You haven't even got a proper mother, although it looks like your father is about to test-run another."

"There is little difference, Miss Lucy," said the doll from above, "between an ego dependant on cumulative successes and a man in a sinking boat — either way you'd better have a good life-jacket."

Mandi turned her head to see Lucy staring up at the doll's bright new blue eyes and charred face. The precious little rich girl squealed a sound of disgust. "What is that thing?"

The distraction was all that Mandi needed. She held the tiny bottle over her cup. She hesitated and glanced up with Lucy at the blue eyes watching her.

Then she turned and emptied the bottle into Lucy's orange juice.

*

Mandi sat on the bed, morning sunlight warm on her legs. She stared at the doll which lay gagged and bound and blinded on the floor. It was a pity; she'd begun to like that doll. But, when it had informed her that it had seen what she'd done, and that it was programmed to report all illegality, she'd been left with no other choice — the designer had no eyes left to poke.

As her dad had sulked around the pavilion after losing yet another competition — second was never good enough for him — Mandi had collected the doll. In the taxi home, her father had comforted himself in the arms of the young woman, while Mandi had kept her palm firmly clamped over the doll's face.

Later, alone in her bedroom, she had wound adhesive tape around the doll's body and mouth and gouged out its new eyes with a nail file, then dumped it on the floor until the morning.

Mandi rolled from the bed and slipped her feet into her winter boots. She stepped over the doll and examined her teeth in the dressing-table mirror. Then she lifted her arms wide and high and slowly raised one knee almost to her chin. Her hands traced fluid figures in the air. Circle left … circle right. In … out. Was this genuine ballet and genuine Tai Chi that her father had choreographed? Was anything genuine? She shrugged her tiny shoulders. It hardly mattered now. So she'd lost yet again. Next year would be different.

Maintaining her elegant stance, she hopped and turned around to face the bed. With a tilt of her head, she glanced below her hovering foot, parted her fine hair with her fingers so she could see, then brought her heel down explosively on the doll's head.

Plastic spat in all directions, pinged off the skirtings, clattered into the corners. The little automaton juddered under her foot, whined, trembled and died. With her heel, Mandi ground the plastic crumbs into the carpet. She picked up the headless body of the doll. It was heavy in her little hand. She straightened out the blackened rag that had once been a smart blue dress.

"I forgot to ask," said Mandi. "Who exactly were you going to tell?"

A woman laughed nearby, in Dad's bedroom, and Mandi smiled.

She knew the woman had slept with her father, but it didn't matter. Mandi would find a way to get rid of this one too. And next year Lucy Aimes would be too old to compete and the prize would be Mandi's.

Then her father would love her. She would have given him what he wanted most … and she couldn't achieve that as a grown-up.

No, it wasn't so bad being a child. Not at all.

She could grow older another year.

GRAVE ROBBERS

Anne Stringer

"Bloody hell," I said as the first fat raindrop splatted on my head.

Leaning on the handle of his rusted old digger, Jasper glanced skyward, not that he could see much in the darkness. "Just a sprinkle," he replied. "Won't amount to nothing."

He was wrong, of course. Within minutes it was a downpour.

"I'm done." Mine had stopped humming as soon as the rain started, and they're bloody hard to use manually. I tossed it out of the hole and climbed up to ground level. My ragged pants were mud from the knee down and sagging from the wet.

Jasper wisely withheld snickers and jokes, though no doubt he had some good ones. He always did. "You can't quit now, Nate. We're almost there! We won't be getting another chance, you know. The system will be back online by morning."

"Bloody well can quit now," I muttered, but relented. "Then you get your skinny arse down there and dig."

He flicked his fag away into the night. Wasn't staying lit in the rain anyhow. Then he dropped into the hole in the ground. His boots squished in the mud, and I could feel cold, wet ooze coming in around my toes. No matter. I'd have all the new boots I wanted soon enough, if Jas knew what he was talking about. Naturally, he swore he did.

"You coming?" he asked, looking up at me. I could barely make out his face in the torchlight. Without waiting for an answer, he flicked the switch on his digger and got to work. And wouldn't you know, it wasn't three times his shovel chewed into the mud and it thunked on something hard.

"Hah!" he crowed, dropping to his knees. "What'd I say, mate? What'd I say?"

"So, it's there. Don't mean there's anything but bones in it."

"We'll just see, won't we?" Eagerly, he cleared mud away from the wood. "C'mon, give us a hand."

I resisted the urge to applaud him and dropped back into the hole. "Damn good thing they don't bury 'em deep no more." We had to clear quite a bit of dirt, and it kept sliding down the sides. We could hardly stay ahead of it. Finally we had enough moved to get at the handles. I climbed up and got the torch so we could have a better look, and shined it down into the hole.

Jas whistled low. "Fancy," he said, touching the scrolled brass. "Bloody funny what folk will put in the ground, ain't it?"

"Open the damn thing. I'm feeling like a half-drowned rat here."

"We'll have a whiskey in a nice warm pub after. How's that?"

It was one of those boxes with a double lid, so he stood on one side and opened the end he figured was the head. Wasn't easy to tell, but he got it right. I moved around to the other side for a better look.

"Don't see any jewels," I said. Just an old decaying body. Even in the rain, the smell was enough to make me sick. I covered my nose with my hand, as if that would help. The fancy satin lining of the box was stained with liquids that leached out of the body. No fancy necklace or tiara, no rings on her withered fingers.

"The word wasn't jewels … exactly," Jasper said, a bit sheepishly. "Treasure is what I heard. It made me think jewels."

She wasn't entirely empty-handed though. She clutched a book in her right hand, and had a cheap plastic rosary wrapped around the fingers of her left. The beads were oversized and joined by string. It looked like something a sped kid would use. Maybe she had some kind of palsy in her later years.

"Well, that's damned disappointing," Jasper said, crouched over her. He knelt in the mud and leaned in, running his hand along her body, feeling around the edges for anything that might have been hidden in there with the corpse. It sent up new waves of decay stink, but he didn't seem to mind. Then he snaked his arm down into the foot end of the coffin, as far as he could reach. It made me gag.

"Let's go have that whiskey." I was pretty disgusted with him by now, in more ways than one. And I was drenched to the bone.

"I ain't leaving with nothing." He wrenched the book free of her grasp, which looked like it was harder than it should have been. The old hag had a grip on it. Then he untangled that crazy rosary, snapping off a couple of fingers in the process.

"C'mon," I groused. "An old bible and a plastic rosary?"

He paused, glaring up at me. "Somewhere else you gotta be?" he said, and I shut up. He tucked the book under his arm, slipped the rosary into a pocket, and climbed out of the hole. We walked away, leaving the grave to fill with water and mud. Jasper didn't even close the lid.

We didn't go to the pub. We were a holy mess and didn't want anybody to know it was us that robbed that grave, even though it got us nothing. Jasper dug the beads out of his pocket and handed them to me. "I'm keeping the book," he said.

"Thanks for nothing," I replied. He went his way and I went mine, under cover of rain and darkness.

Once home, I changed out of my filthy wet clothes, stuck a pan under a roof leak, and brewed a cup of tea. I added a generous splash of whiskey to help shake off the cold, then sat at the table with my share of the treasure. It didn't seem Jasper's book was going to be any more valuable than this, but then people put interesting things in their bibles. I was going to have to make sure he didn't try to put anything past me.

The rosary was an odd thing, all right. The things some people think are precious! I couldn't get a crust of bread for this. What a wasted night's work.

It seemed a bit heavy for plastic though, which gave me an idea. I found a small hammer and tapped on one of the beads until it cracked. Then I wedged a knife blade into the crack and pried it apart. There was something sparkly in there. I almost cut my finger in my eagerness to get at it.

Finally I got the thing to break apart and a little red faceted gem spilled out onto the table. Ruby, or garnet, or maybe just glass? I didn't know. But why go to such effort to hide coloured glass? I went to work on the rest of the beads.

Hours later, I had a pile of ruined plastic and scattered sparklies on the table. My tea was cold, but I gulped it down so as not to waste the whiskey. I'd done pretty well, I thought. Not all of the beads had something in them, but a lot of them did. There was one that looked like an opal that had broken, but the rest were in good shape. I couldn't wait to tell Jasper. I got up from the table and reached for my jacket.

But then I thought it over. For all he knew, I had a worthless trinket of plastic and string. Why should I tell him any different? Anyway, it was still raining out. I decided to sleep on it. I gathered the gems up in a hankie and stuffed them under my mattress, and sleep on it I did.

The next day brought an end to the rain, but no sun. I'd decided to take one of the gems to a fence I knew and trusted, at least as much as you can trust anybody these days. No sense making a fuss if it turned out to be cheap paste. I picked the red one, wrapped up the rest and stashed them under a loose floorboard in the corner, a spot I kept my valuables. It'd been mostly empty for a long time.

Old Frankie hobbled out from behind his counter when he saw me come in. His shop was dusty and cluttered, filled with an odd assortment of cheap trash. Broken dollies he was trying to fix, musical instruments missing strings or other vital parts, toasters and televisions that probably hadn't worked in years. Little knick-knacks like you might see sitting on doilies in an old lady's cottage, statues of cats or sad-faced children. Weapons decorated the wall behind the counter, along with his posted licence allowing him to sell them. A glass-top case held jewellery and watches, mostly cheap costume stuff. Once in a while there was a real treasure to be found in that shop too. Frankie was a clever one. He knew the value of everything in there, and he'd let some things go for a song sometimes. Let people think he was addled and they were pulling something over on him. It got him a lot of repeat customers, and it kept suspicion off his illegal activities.

"Got something for you to look at, Frankie." I unwrapped the gem, holding it in the hankie on my palm for him to inspect.

"Hmm," was all he said, grabbing a loupe off the counter and fitting it to his eye. First he just looked at it this way and that, and then he tapped a switch on the side. "Dam, boy," he said finally, switching off the loupe. He set it back on the counter and looked up at me. "You got yourself a nice little ruby there."

That's the thing about old Frankie. He might be stingy with his offers, but he wouldn't lie to me about what he saw.

"Yeah?" I said. "What's it worth?"

"Where'd you get it?" he countered.

I shrugged. "Lifted it off an old lady." True enough.

"The fuzz was here this morning." He glanced at the gem again. I could see he wanted it. "They were looking for items that might've been stolen out of a grave. Said old lady Farnsworth was dug up last night."

"No shit," I said, hoping I sounded disinterested. I appreciated the head's up though.

Then he took another look, increasing the mag on the loupe. "It's marked."

"Bloody hell." My dreams of the easy life went up in smoke, just like that. Nobody would buy marked goods, and if I was caught with them…

"I might know a buyer who won't care."

"Come now, Frankie. Who's not gonna care if they're marked? Nowhere on Earth that'll pass."

He smiled and waggled his brows at me.

"You mean-"

"Indeed I do, boy, indeed I do."

He offered me an amount, I countered, we haggled and settled. The codger enjoyed the game and I went along. He always came out ahead, but I wasn't about to begrudge him. He was a good man to know and I wanted to stay in his favour. I stuffed the cash in my pocket and headed out. He went back behind the counter and was studying the gem with his fancy loupe when I left.

I had to tell Jasper. We were partners, after all, and if I didn't old Frankie probably would. Not that I had to tell him everything though. I headed for the pub, the most likely spot to find Jasper even this early in the day.

He was at our usual spot, a booth in a dim corner. A glass of something on ice sat next to his elbow, but his head was bent over a book. Comical really. I wouldn't call him a reader. I slid in across from him. He ignored me until I picked up his glass and took a drink.

But he didn't object, like he normally would. "Nate," was all he said, and then went back to his book.

If that's how he was going to be… I picked up the glass again and set it on my side of the table. "Found Jesus, have you?"

"Hmm?" He looked up again. "Oh, this. No, it ain't a bible. I don't know what the hell it is. What do you make of this?

He turned the book around and showed me the page that'd had him mesmerized. It was like those optical illusion things, where the pictures look like they're moving or you're supposed to see something different in them. Only it was script.

I blinked and shook my head. "Giving me a bloody headache," I said, and picked up the glass again, mostly so I wouldn't see that page.

But he set the book down and went back to staring at it. That's when I noticed that this book was in pristine condition, which was odd considering where it'd been.

"There's something here," Jas muttered, but it didn't seem like he was talking to me. "I've almost got it. I'm this close…"

"Mm," I said, swallowing nearly half the contents of the glass with one gulp. "Say, Jas, I've some news."

"Yeah?" he said, not bothering to look up from the book.

"Yeah. You know that rosary?"

"Huh?"

I'd lost him already. I put my hand over the open page he was absorbed in and he glared over the book at me.

"What the fuck you want?"

"The rosary."

"What rosary?"

Jesus, give me strength. "The rosary the old lady had. Remember?" I nodded toward the book. "The old lady with the book."

"Right," he said, and grinned. Clearly he thought I'd been screwed in that deal, and he wasn't suffering any guilt over it.

I leaned closer. The place was mostly empty, but it wouldn't do to be overheard. "It isn't just plastic in those beads."

"It ain't? So what are they?"

"The old bag's jewels. She had 'em encased."

"Huh. No shit." The wanger was going back to his book. I just gave him the greatest news of our illustrious career in crime, and he'd rather look at sodding pictures!

"I'm worried about you, mate." I downed the rest of his drink and raised a finger at the bartender for another. Just one. If Jasper was going to ignore me, I wasn't going to buy his liquor.

"What do you make of this?" he asked, sliding the open book over to me.

"Nothing," I said, and slammed the damned thing shut.

"Bloody hell!" Suddenly he was nearly shouting. "You didn't even look, and now I've lost the page!"

I couldn't help but laugh. "Lost the page? Have you gone mental? The pages are all the same!"

He gave me a look that was pure disgust. "Don't be an idiot, Nate. You and your sped rosary." Then he opened the book again and started leafing through.

The girl brought the drink over and I downed it in a single gulp. It was watered down mild, which was to be expected, especially at this price. Getting up, I pulled some wadded cred from my pocket and dropped it on the table. "Your share," I said. "And some to cover the booze."

He nodded but left it lying there, like he hadn't even noticed it. Cred at his elbow, and his nose in a book. This was not the Jasper I knew. I left him puzzling over scribbled lines and walked out. The waitress was already eyeing the money.

*

I didn't see him for a few days after that. I'd heard nothing more about the police looking for grave robbers, so I went to see old Frankie again. I took a little blue gem this time.

He was eager to see it. His buyer, he said, would take anything he could get his hands on. He wouldn't say how he had contacts among the notoriously secretive alien visitors, or what they would want with Earth rocks, however pretty they might be, but I got him to come up on the price a bit and told him I'd be in touch if I got wind of anything more. Frankie's a decent enough sort, but nobody's completely trustworthy these days. He wouldn't outright rob a source, bad for business, yet I couldn't be sure he'd be above hiring some anonymous B&E. Damn shame, really.

Once again I considered keeping it from Jasper, but my conscience got the better of me. I found him at the pub again, hunched over the book.

"You look like hell, mate," I said after the girl took my order. He did too. He looked thinner and older somehow. "Been sick?"

"You can't have it," he snarled at me, snapping the book shut and sliding it off the table to his lap.

"Easy. I don't want the bloody thing." I dropped some cred notes on the table. "That's yours," I said. "Why don't you buy some food? Looks like you ain't been eating. And get some sleep, for crissake."

"You'd like that." He grabbed the money and pocketed it. Then he seemed to shake off his mood when the girl came with whiskey for us both. "Nothin' personal, Nate," he said by way of apology. "There are people who want the book. I have to guard it every second."

"You're sounding paranoid."

"Not a bit," he countered. "See that old gent behind you?"

I glanced over my shoulder. It was early in the day and so the place was pretty quiet. There was a man sitting behind me, his face buried in a newspaper. Not so old, it seemed. No older than me. I turned back to Jasper. "Yeah, so?"

"He's done nothing but stare at me all morning."

I glanced again, but the fellow hadn't moved. I shrugged. "If you say so."

He downed the whiskey in one swallow, grabbed the book and tucked it under his arm, and left without so much as a see-you-later. I followed him out and saw him snarling at random people he passed by. When a young man took a swing at him, he wrapped both arms around the book, ducked and ran.

That was the last time I ever saw him at the pub, which was damn odd. The place had been like a second home as long as I knew him.

I nearly wrote him off then. He wasn't the Jasper who'd been a mate since we were boys. I didn't see him for days, and I was doing just fine on my own. Never better. Curiosity got the better of me though. I picked up some fish and chips to take along, as it hadn't looked like he'd been eating much, and it gave me an excuse to pop by.

The house looked deserted, but that was nothing new. He'd done little to keep it up since his gran died. I banged on the door a couple of times before he responded.

"Bugger off!" he yelled from within.

"Jas, it's me. Nate. Open up."

The door opened, just a crack. "What'n hell do you want?"

"Lemme in." I held up the package. "I brought food."

The door opened just a bit wider. He glanced behind him. "Ain't a good time, mate."

"Why?" I asked, craning to see past him. "Having a party and didn't invite me?"

My attempt at making light didn't go over well. "Bugger off," he said again, stepping back to close the door.

But I put my hand on it to stop him. "C'mon, Jas. I just came by to see if you're all right. You ain't been out."

He glanced back inside, into the gloom of the house, and then stepped out onto the stoop. "They followed me home, mate," he whispered. "But I'm taking care of it."

"Who followed you?"

"You know. The old gent from the pub. Old lady Farnsworth."

"Jas … old lady Farnsworth is dead. Remember? We dug her up." I was worried, clearly he'd taken leave of his senses, but trying hard to be calm and reasonable.

"I know! But she's in there right now!"

"So, what is it you're doing?" I tried to hand him the package, but he ignored it.

"The book showed me the way. I've got to get back to it."

"Jas." I put a hand on his shoulder. "Come on. Let's go to the pub, I'll buy you a brew."

"No!" he shouted, pulling away from me. "That's just what they want me to do!"

"Let's burn the book. I bet they'll go away then. Or give it to me and-"

"You're one of them!" His eyes got wide and he back away from me, fumbled with the doorknob, and ducked back into his house. "You can't have it!"

I sighed. "Jas, come on. You're not being rational."

"Sod off!" He slammed the door and threw the bolt.

I saw a flash from within and stepped over to the window for a look. I had to brush away dust and spider webs first, and then lean close because it was so dark in there. The first thing I saw was a small flame in the centre of the floor, rising up from the open book. Good, I thought. He's burning the damn thing. Only then did it occur that the whole house would go up with it, so I figured Jasper was going to need a rescue.

The flame grew and started changing colours, like some really weird chemicals were on those pages. That would explain quite a lot about Jasper's behaviour. First it was green, then flashed purple, then blue. With each colour change it grew. It settled on a quite lovely lavender hue. White sparks shot up the column of flame and then stopped, floating there. Like two eyes. Fanciful thinking, I guess, but that's what it reminded me of.

By the light of this fire I could see more of the room. There was Jasper, standing with his head bowed. His lips were moving, but I couldn't hear what he was saying. And then, looking past him, I saw others. A little girl in a nightdress. An old gent leaning on a cane. Old lady Farnsworth.

I must've made some noise, because they looked up. I stumbled back a step from the window and Jasper looked up. Then the eyes in the fire turned and looked right at me. The package fell from my hands, and I ran for my life. The thought of being alone in my flat was terrifying, so I went to the pub instead and got drunk enough to convince myself I hadn't seen any of it.

Old Frankie came in, sat with me for a bit, but I was too far gone to pay him much mind. When he told me his buyers wanted more, and had asked him about a book, it only made me drink faster. I'm not even sure how I made it home that night. Maybe Frankie helped, maybe he's stronger than he looks. Maybe he searched my place when I was passed out too. I woke up in my own bed though, so I made it there somehow. The hangover headache kept my mind occupied most of the day.

I couldn't sleep that night though. I knew I was going to have to go back.

In the full light of day, that's what I did. It was the same old run-down cottage I remembered. Jasper had grown up there. So had I, in truth, since I spent more of my childhood there than in my own house. It didn't look nearly so frightening now as it had in the dark with that purple glow coming from the windows.

I knocked, then banged on the door but got no answer. I tried the knob yet it was locked up tight. So then I went to the window where I'd stood the night before last. The food was still there where I'd dropped it, torn open and partially eaten by dogs, most likely.

It looked very ordinary inside as well. No fire, no ghostly faces, just shabby furniture and worn carpet. And Jasper, lying still in the centre of the room.

I rang up the police, told them I thought he might be injured, and waited for them to come. They made me stay outside while they went in. They called for the coroner straight away. Jasper was dead, and had been for at least a day.

"Electrocuted, apparently, poor fellow. These old places and their wiring! Lucky it didn't burn it down. He must've sent up some right sparks."

Was it possible that's what I'd witnessed? Maybe if I was drunk enough I could convince myself of that.

They'd decided there was no foul play, or at least didn't care if there was, so they let me go in. Jasper lay crumpled on his side, one arm outstretched, the blackened fingers near the electrical cord to the telly. There were black streaks on the wall above the outlet too. Next to his body lay his precious book, closed now, not a mark on it. I picked it up.

The cover was quite ornate, deep purple with designs pressed into the leather. I opened it. The pages were pristine. Page one was a swirling mass of colour, lovely and mesmerizing. The next page had flowing script, and while the form was unfamiliar to me, I knew that if I studied it enough, in time its meaning would become clear and some great secrets would be revealed.

"Take it with you, if you like," said a quavering old-woman voice. I glanced up from the book into the sad eyes of old lady Farnsworth. She nodded and smiled encouragement.

I snapped the book closed and dropped it onto Jasper's body.

"What do you suggest we do with that?" asked the policeman.

"Bury it with him," I said.

But I made sure I knew where his grave was.

FATHER'S LAST RIDE

Aliette de Bodard

Ruth Elemanis was putting the last touches to her 3-D animation when the house AI spoke through her implants. Visitor, it said.

Not many people came to Ruth's apartment, especially not in the middle of the afternoon. Ruth, puzzled, asked for a video overlay. A shimmering image appeared in the middle of her field of vision, superimposed on the familiar setting of her living room: a man, standing hesitantly on her doorstep.

"Ruth?" he was asking. "Can I come in?"

It took her a moment to identify him. The face and the voice were familiar, but she could not place him at first.

Javier.

What was he doing here? She'd only ever seen him on video feeds with her father, moments before they started a ride: both of them fully attired in foil suits, both of their faces transfigured by their eagerness to enter the aurora, to speed on their lightskimmers through the curtains of shimmering light above the northern hemisphere of Silica. Now Javier just looked pitifully small and wan.

She opened the door and invited him in. He came to a stop in the centre of her living room, refusing to meet her gaze. There were grey circles under his eyes. "Ruth... I came to say how sorry I am. We did all we could, but we couldn't find him."

Something tightened in her chest. "What do you mean?"

"You don't know?" Javier's voice was puzzled. "It's your father—"

It had to be her father. Why else would Javier be here? "He's dead, isn't he?" she asked. She wondered why she felt so numb, so removed; but of course her father had run away, had abandoned his own family when Ruth was still a child. He had been out of touch for twenty years—save for that brief, awkward

59

lunch they'd had a week ago. He was a stranger to her.

"He didn't come back," Javier said. "He entered the aurora at 2200 hours, but he never came out. We waited and waited, and then we went back into the auroral zone, hoping we'd find something, anything."

"I see," Ruth said. "And you didn't?"

"It was Central who found his lightskimmer," Javier explained. "Through the emergency beacon. It was drifting in the upper layers of the atmosphere. The EM shield had absorbed too much energy: it was burnt through. So were most components of the lightskimmer. Central retrieved only the core routines from the memory banks."

"There must have been a body," Ruth said, and then berated herself for the stupidity of that remark.

Javier shrugged. "He was dead by that time, Ruth."

"How would you know?"

His voice was gentle. "When his EM shield went down in the aurora, he would have taken an electrical current of several thousand amperes. No one survives that."

"I see," Ruth said, which was all she could think to say. "Why wasn't I told, Javier?"

He still wouldn't look at her. "Your mother is his next-of-kin, so she would have been notified as soon as Central finished the procedures. This morning, probably. The other people on the kin list get notified later. Ruth, I'm sorry—"

Ruth turned away from him. She stared through the huge window pane of her apartment at the city spread out below her fifty-second floor. Letheria was close to the North Pole: it was already night. She could see no aurora—too many lights from the city would mask its glow. "It's 1600 hours, Javier," she said, tonelessly. "She hasn't called."

"Obviously not," Javier said. "I thought she'd at least tell you. I know she had no love for aurora riders, but still—"

Ruth shook her head. He had no idea how much her mother hated the aurora riders like Javier, the men who had lured her husband away from her, into that insane venture.

"I'd have come sooner if I'd known," Javier said finally. "He didn't have much to leave you. He'd willed his lightskimmer to you a while back, but you can't salvage a lot out of it now. You could call Central if you want it back."

"I don't want his lightskimmer," Ruth snapped, turning back to him. She thought back to her lunch with her father. She had stared at him as he'd sat down, at this middle-aged man who no longer meant anything to her. She had wondered why she'd agreed to see him again. He hadn't had much to say to her either, and they'd parted on an impersonal goodbye. "Why, Javier?" she asked. "Why did it have to happen?"

His face was set. "Aurora-riding is dangerous, Ruth. Your mother must have told you that enough times. He must have forgotten one last check, must have misread his shield's gauge—must have missed a safety warning from the lightskimmer—"

"Balderdash," Ruth scoffed. "He'd been doing this for twenty years. He wouldn't have been so careless." He'd loved aurora-riding more than his own family. Enough to abandon them, she thought, but quashed the notion before it could become bitter.

Javier stared at her for a while. At last he said, angrily, "What answer do you want, Ruth? Do you want me to say it was suicide? It would be a lie. That past week, I'd never seen him so glad to be alive."

That past week. Since that awkward lunch. It had meant something to her father then, she thought with an odd feeling of elation, soon extinguished when she remembered he was dead. How could you? she thought, and she wasn't sure whether she meant his death, or his earlier abandonment of her and her mother. Whichever way, her father could not answer her.

Javier was looking at her with concern. Suddenly, she felt tired of his solicitude, of the way grief weighed down every one of his words. "Javier," she said. "I'm sorry. I'm very grateful to you for coming to tell me, but could you leave? I need—" Time. Time to take all of this in. Time to grieve.

Javier nodded. At the door, he paused. "Call me if you need anything," he said.

And then he left.

*

Once alone, Ruth called on the house AI to retrieve her mails. There was nothing new from her father—what did she expect, a message from beyond death?—or her mother. She quickly reread the mail her father had sent her on the morning of his death. His last mail. She asked her implants to overlay her field of vision with it so she could read. In it he thanked her, stiffly, for the lunch and the gift she'd sent him that morning—a copy of her latest 3-D animation: a landscape of Letheria with the aurora barely hinted at in the background.

He was dead.

She could not quite believe it. Her father hadn't been there to see her grow, but she'd always had the certainty that he was alive, laughing as his lightskimmer speeded above Silica. The certainty that he'd send pictures and video feeds of the aurora from time to time, which her mother would erase from the house network, tears of rage in her eyes.

Dead.

And she'd known nothing of it.

She stared for a while at the stark walls of her apartment, composing herself. And then she called her mother.

At first she saw nothing, heard nothing but the random, hissing noise of optical communications. Then her mother's voice spoke, harsh: "Lights."

The shimmering, half-transparent image of her mother stood in the middle of Ruth's living room. She still wore her civil service uniform; Ruth guessed she had just returned from work.

"Ruth," her mother said. "You don't call often these days."

"No," Ruth said. The easy camaraderie she and her mother had shared during Ruth's childhood and adolescence was gone. Now, every time Ruth called, it was the same: the conversation degenerated into a string of reproaches. Her mother only needed an excuse to voice her disappointment on Ruth's choice of career. Ruth said, as calmly as she could, "Father's dead. And you know."

Her mother's face did not move. "Yes."

"When were you planning on telling me? Tomorrow, when they finished the procedure and you couldn't hide it any more?" She couldn't keep the hurt, the anger from her voice. She didn't try.

Her mother crossed her arms over her chest. Her gaze, remote, expressionless, must have been the same she turned on her underlings in the civil service when they'd failed her. "It wouldn't have hurt you to wait a little more," she said at last.

"He's my father!"

Her mother said quietly, "He is nothing. He's no longer part of this family."

"That's what you believe? Then why didn't you find someone else, after all those years? Why didn't you get a divorce?"

Her mother turned her head slightly. The change of light revealed tears, glinting near her neural implants. She said, as if she hadn't heard Ruth's question, "He was such a fool, your father. He had a brilliant mind, but no ambition. He couldn't face his own responsibilities. And, in the end, he ran away to the only place where nothing would impose on him."

"Mother—"

"It's the truth." Her mother's voice was quieter now, almost spent. "I always thought he'd come back, you know. That one day he'd walk through that door as if nothing had ever happened. What a fool I was to believe in him."

"He died," Ruth said, taken aback by her mother's words. "He didn't do it to spite you."

Her mother's face twisted. "You knew nothing of him. Do you think you can stand here and tell me to my face what kind of man he was?"

"He can't have been—"

She cut Ruth off. "You know nothing. He was irresponsible, unreliable. And, despite my best efforts to bring you up as a responsible daughter, he's influenced you. That wish of yours to become a digital artist—foolishness, girl. You were such a brilliant child, you placed in all the examinations..."

"Mother," Ruth cut in, trying to stop the flow of words. "I'm doing what I want to." She knew that argument wouldn't work.

"Nonsense. Your place is in the civil service, not dreaming up those computer-aided fantasies. You're lucky to make a living at all out of that."

"Father's dead!" Ruth said, as forcefully as she could. "Can't you at least have some respect for him, even if it's for thirty seconds?"

Her mother glared at her. "Is that all you wanted to say?"

It was, more or less—since this conversation, as usual, was going nowhere. But Ruth, remembering her father's mail, said, "You're next-of-kin. Central has turned all access rights to his personal folder over to you."

Her mother laughed bitterly. "And you want them? Fine. I'll transfer them to you as soon as this communication is over. There's nothing I want from him."

Ruth didn't know what else she could say, so she thanked her mother and ended the conversation. Alone again, she took a deep breath, trying to calm herself. And failing.

She checked her mails again. Her mother, true to her word, had lost no time in granting Ruth full access rights to her father's personal folder. Surprisingly, it wasn't on the Letheria network, but on the Konos one. Konos? Konos was a city on the edge of the equatorial desert that covered most of Silica. It produced electronic components. Why would her father go there?

With the help of a data-mining program, it took Ruth fifteen minutes to extract the information. The trivial first: that her father had been living in Konos when he had met her mother, that he'd held a string of odd jobs before they'd moved to Letheria, and that his job as tutor to the upper class of Letheria had lasted barely three years. Lack of drive, the lay-off slip noted.

The subfolder marked 'personal' yielded nothing but image upon image of the auroras: breathtaking videos of light, taken at the huge speed of a lights-kimmer; light that shifted from bright green to red over the dark background of space. Sometimes her father had managed to catch a glimpse of a Ghost herd, the wedge-shaped aliens basking in the influx of energy from the aurora's magnetic field. The videos had that strange, ethereal beauty her father's pictures always had, the beauty Ruth couldn't recreate in her art.

The last video wasn't of the aurora. It was the animation she'd sent him: the tall glass buildings of Letheria, shivering in the light, thrusting towards the barely-seen aurora, as if the whole city were seeking a way towards the light. Ruth stared at it, her eyes stinging, wondering why her father had put it with the others. It had no place there.

Last of all were two things. One proved, beyond doubt, that her mother hadn't checked the contents of the subfolders: it was the access code to her father's bank account. Curious, Ruth entered it, and stared at the impossible numbers that appeared. So much money flowing in—most, but not all of it, going into repairs of the lightskimmer. All the transactions were from the same sources: the extra-planetary agencies that bought her father's videos of the Ghosts, wanting to study the aliens but not to take the risk or the expense of launching a craft into the aurora. Ruth hadn't thought aurora-riding could bring in so much money—but of course her father had to have lived on something during those twenty years.

And, last of all, she retrieved something that Central must have added for her mother's benefit: her father's flight-plan, recovered from the lightskimmer. Nothing particular, a wide circle within the auroral zone, until the lightskimmer came to a stop close to the North Pole, and then went on, rudderless, plunging towards the atmosphere of Silica. The automatic stabilizing systems had finally brought the trajectory back to horizontal. By then, of course, her father wasn't on board any more.

Why? Ruth wondered, and thought of the lunch again. The lunch her father had asked for. He'd sat as she recounted her life, his face unreadable.

Her mother's voice said, in her mind, He couldn't face his own responsibilities. He ran away.

He couldn't face his own daughter.

No.

It wasn't that. It couldn't be that.

*

Late at night, Ruth finished watching the videos of the aurora. She called Javier, who, not surprisingly, wasn't at home. He was out, riding the auroras. Ruth left a terse message and went to bed.

Her sleep was restless, broken by images from the videos she'd watched in the evening: the aurora slowly coming into focus, curtains of vivid green light replacing the grey sky of twilight; the Ghosts slowly gathering to revel in the electromagnetic energy; the lightskimmers with their frail riders entering it one by one, and never coming back.

Whatever her mother had told her, those pictures said otherwise. Ben Elemanis hadn't only been running away; the aurora had been his passion.

Waking up alone in her bed, she stared at the dark sky above Letheria. A memory would not leave her: the evening her father had come home, having just lost his job.

She'd been seven then, wholly ensconced in her behavioural studies, hoping, like her mother, to be accepted into the civil service. When she heard her father's voice, she'd unplugged herself from her learning program and crept into the hallway. They were in the kitchen; but in the silence of the apartment their voices carried over to where she was standing.

"'Lack of drive'. You didn't even invest yourself in that job. Have I wasted my time?" her mother had asked.

"You just don't understand," her father had said. He sounded wan, defeated.

"I understand you're not making any effort. Do you think you can drift through life with no idea of where you're going?"

"I know where I'm going. I wanted a family."

"You have one. Provide for it."

"You're doing that already," her father said angrily. "Quite adequately, and without my help. I'm not needed here."

"Not needed?" Her mother's voice rose. "Is that your excuse for shirking your responsibilities? You're such a fool, Ben. You're so smart, and it's all going to waste. You could have had such a good career—"

"I'm not your pet," her father said. "I'm not your project. And Ruth..."

"Leave Ruth out of it," her mother snapped.

"Leave her? Then let's talk about me. I did what you wanted. I took the job you offered me, and found that all it did was make me miserable. Now I'll make my own way."

Her mother's answer was cold, cutting. "Then you're no longer part of this house."

There was silence then. The words flowed over Ruth, settled in the hollow of her stomach. Surely her father would have something to say, some words to make it better. But he'd said softly, "That's the way you're playing it? Fine. Then I'll leave."

And he had. Oh, he hadn't left immediately; he'd lingered a while, like a spectre in the apartment, looking at Ruth but never speaking to her. Looking at his wife and making the barest attempts at conversation. But in the end, he'd taken his things and left. Her mother had said nothing. She'd removed every trace of his passage from the house, expressionless. But Ruth had seen her one evening, crying bitterly in the kitchen, sure that she was alone and that no one would witness that show of weakness. Ruth had said nothing, had only buried herself in her studies, hoping to forget.

To the adult Ruth, who sat on her bed twenty years later, looking back at that fateful quarrel, it seemed all the unsaid things between her parents had been aired that night; the root of their fundamental disagreement laid bare.

Your excuse for shirking your responsibilities.

I'm not your pet.

Her house AI was speaking in her ear, insistently. Incoming call from Javier Hernandez.

Javier.

Ruth put on a dressing gown and took the call. The image of Javier, shimmering, half-transparent, was overlaid on the familiar setting of her sitting room.

He stood, swaying, his face pale, his eyes bloodshot. Ruth said sharply, "You've just come back from a ride, haven't you?"

He smiled. "It was a good one. Ten hours chasing the aurora. Ben would have liked it."

"It's not what I meant," Ruth retorted, not sure she wanted to hear more about her father's passion.

"I know," Javier said. "I wanted to return your call."

"It's not ... urgent," Ruth said. Her father wouldn't come back.

"Tell me." Javier sat down on his sofa. His bloodshot eyes were intent.

Ruth hesitated, then forwarded him her father's flight path. "That was his lightskimmer's trajectory. I wanted to know if there was anything unusual."

Javier sat still, no doubt staring at the flight log through his implants. He said at last, "No, nothing much. It's rather short, even for half an hour."

"Short?"

"His speed would have been maybe sixty kilometres per hour. A lightskimmer averages seven times that." He frowned. "Also, it's pretty close to the North Pole. Unusual."

"Why?"

"It's all about the speed," Javier said. "Lightskimmers aren't very manoeuvrable. With an arc that narrow, he wouldn't have had long stretches to accelerate."

"That's unusual?"

"It is for me. For him... I don't know. We don't check each other's trajectories. Once you're in the aurora, you're your own man. I guess that's one of the reasons it appealed to him."

He was shrewd. Too much perhaps. Ruth wasn't ready to have her father dissected.

"So it's not natural?"

"I didn't say that," Javier said. "Perhaps he didn't want speed. Perhaps he wanted to take pictures of Ghosts; they're usually not far from the Pole."

"And the Ghosts might have harmed him?"

He shook his head. "Ghosts are harmless. They're just pulsing organisms of jelly that convert the electrical currents into energy. They've never attacked a rider; they've never even tried to communicate with us. They feed on the aurora, night after night, until it burns them to death."

"I don't need a biology lesson," Ruth protested, entranced in spite of herself.

She called up her father's flight log again, stared at the red lines overlaid on her field of vision. "Javier?" she asked. "I want to ride the aurora."

He raised an eyebrow. "It's no place for novices."

"I know it's not safe," Ruth said. "But I want to see what he saw every night." She didn't add what she also wanted to do: retrace her father's path through the aurora, hoping for an explanation for his death.

Though Javier protested for a while, in the end, she finally convinced him.

*

It took Ruth three months to prepare herself: to acquire, with her father's money, a middle-of-the-range lightskimmer, a foil suit and an EM shield, and to train herself to fly it, with Javier's help. She applied for a lightskimmer licence, and barely scraped enough points to pass the manoeuvring exam.

After her licence, Javier insisted on training her further; finally he pronounced her ready—but still installed an auto-pilot program in her lightskimmer's memory. "Just in case," he said, and he wasn't smiling.

On the day of the ride, Javier came to collect her at 1530 hours.

"I checked the solar forecast," he said as they took a commuter shuttle to the north of the city, to the lightskimmer landing strip. "There's a peak of magnetic activity due shortly after 1700 hours. It should trigger a nice aurora here. Are you sure you're ready?"

Ruth, her oxygen mask on her knees, shrugged. "I suppose."

Her implants switched networks twice during the journey: once to North Letheria services, and then to the emergency band. After the second switch, Javier said, "Let me see the references on your implants."

Ruth accessed her personal folder and forwarded him the file with the numbers of her implants. Javier sat still for a while, his eyes distant, no doubt comparing what she'd given him with something of his own.

"They're all optical," he noted. "Good. Otherwise you'd have had to switch them off. The magnetic field in the aurora plays havoc with anything electronic."

Ruth smiled without joy. "My mother believed I should have the best tech available."

Javier made no comment on that.

When they arrived, twilight had deepened into night. On the landing strip, dozens of lightskimmers were parked side by side, shining under the neon lights. Her lightskimmer was waiting for her at the end of the line, a sleek, flat-bottomed craft, open at the top. A crowd of other riders had gathered around it, watching her with hostility.

"Who's this?" one burly man asked Javier.

"Ruth Elemanis," Javier said. "Old Ben's daughter."

The man stared at her. "Ain't no place for girls still wet behind the ears," he snapped.

Ruth returned the gaze levelly. "I'm quite capable of taking care of myself," she said, and walked past him.

Overhead, as the darkness became complete, the aurora appeared: a long arc of reddish light stretching from east to west, quivering as if eager to expand.

Javier helped her lie down on the floor of the lightskimmer; he showed her, again, how to grasp the handles so that the chemical pads on her gloves would stick.

"Don't forget. Check your shield gauge. It will absorb energy, but its capacity isn't infinite. When it becomes red, it's time to leave before you get fried," he said.

"You've said it a thousand times," Ruth said, shaking her head.

"Because it's important," Javier insisted. He smiled. "Don't worry. I've seen many things, but we've never lost a novice."

"You lost my father," she said, before she could think.

His gaze was serious for a moment. "He was no novice. He was riding the auroras long before I ever came here." He paused, stared at her as if trying to read her mind. "He was proud of you," he said finally. "He would have been even prouder if he could see you now."

Ruth said nothing. She stared at the plexiglass visor that occupied the front of the lightskimmer. Javier left her to settle in his own craft. The oxygen flow started coming through her mask; she inhaled, deeply, trying to calm herself. Soon, all too soon, the other lightskimmers lifted from the ground; and only she and Javier remained.

She heard his voice, relayed through the optical communication system. "Ruth? It's time."

He'd ingrained the gesture in her by now: she pressed both hands on the handles and twisted clockwise. She heard the motors' hum beneath her, and an involuntary thrill ran through her body.

The lightskimmer rose, swiftly, gaining speed as it ascended. The whole structure started to vibrate under her, and then the buffers kicked in, dampening the oscillations.

Javier said, "Look at it. Isn't it beautiful?"

Under her, in the darkness, lay the northern hemisphere of Silica: the crowded cities near the North Pole with their skyscrapers of glass, the flatlands gradually giving way to the desert and its electronic plants. Ruth held her breath. She had no words for Javier. "Yes," she said at last.

The altitude was overlaid over her field of vision. She watched it increase. Ten kilometres. Thirty.

Fifty, sixty.

They were arcing towards the aurora now; it filled their eyes with its dancing rays. Some riders had already peeled away from the formation, entering the display at a different place. Most of them were accelerating; among them was Javier.

Ruth had spent some time configuring the autopilot Javier had installed for her. It was not doing quite what he'd intended. Instead of accelerating her lightskimmer, it was imperceptibly slowing her down, separating her from the rest of the riders.

As she grew closer to the aurora, its splendour filled her field of vision. Her EM shield came to life with an audible snap, a shimmering veil of light, barely visible, that would protect her from the strong electromagnetic field within the aurora.

She was inside now, enfolded in red light. Silence had fallen as she climbed higher; now it was broken by an occasional electric crackle.

The lines of the magnetic field appeared in bright yellow inside her visor; she erased them from the display. They didn't belong in the aurora.

"Ruth?" Javier called through her com system angrily. His own lightskimmer was already too far away to be seen; and Ruth knew how hard the crafts were to manoeuvre. It would be quite a while before he could slow down enough to turn around. "What do you think you're doing?"

"Making my own way," Ruth replied. "Don't worry about me."

"I'm responsible for you. You're not going off on your own."

"You can't prevent me," Ruth said. "I'll be careful."

"Careful? You don't know what there is to be careful about. I'm slowing down now," Javier declared.

"You can," Ruth said, "and you can turn around, eventually. But then you'll have to find where I've gone."

"I will, never fear," Javier answered. Even through the low-quality communication, she could hear his annoyance, tinged with wry amusement. "You're your father's daughter, Ruth. No doubt about that."

And then there was silence. Ruth cut off her communication, not wanting to hear Javier again. She had some time before he came back; more than enough, surely, for her need.

She called up the flight log, stared again at the narrow arc, passing so close to the North Pole. No space to accelerate, Javier had said.

No, her father had been looking for something else.

Ruth had set the autopilot to reproduce her father's trajectory; she tried to relax. Every muscle in her body felt stiff from the unnatural position.

Around her, the aurora was deepening. Whole areas of the sky shifted from red to yellow-green. The light, seen from closer, was glorious: shades unseen on Silica, merging into one another, shivering as if on the verge of collapse—and yet holding on, minute after minute.

Her lightskimmer cut through the aurora, going at the same speed as her father: a slow, ponderous circuit that allowed her to fill her eyes and her mind to the point of bursting. Compared to that, her art was nothing, the scrawls of a blind child.

Javier's words came back to her. He was so proud of you.

Her father had never shown any interest in her. After he left home, he'd never come back...

No, wait. That wasn't true. Her mind, busily dredging up old memories, conjured up an instant that had since long faded into oblivion.

He'd come back, late one night, two years after leaving. There'd been some argument between him and her mother—not unusual.

Some argument... She couldn't remember. She'd been plugged into the network, studying for her law exam, worrying that she'd never make the cut. Scraps of dialogue had made their way to her, in the rare moments when the AI wasn't blaring practise questions into her mind.

I've come to have my say... You don't leave her a chance either...

Her mother's voice, harsh, unyielding. I'm ensuring her future.

She's not yours either...You can't mould her as you wish...

He was so proud of you.

So proud to learn she hadn't entered the civil service in the end, that she'd stood up and rejected all her mother had tried to force on her. That she was an artist and that her animation, the one she'd sent him, had hints of beauty, the bare bones compared to what was now unfolding before her.

She let her lightskimmer cut through the aurora, her eyes dry. The light around her had started to form patterns: curls and waves like those of an ocean. No wonder her father had found such pleasure in riding the aurora. He hadn't been there for the speed or the thrill of danger.

He'd been there for the sheer beauty of it.

Her lightskimmer slowed to a stop; she'd reached the end of her father's trajectory. At this point, he'd already tumbled down into the atmosphere below, his EM shield shattered.

And then it came to Ruth, with a chill that seemed to make her whole suit shiver, that it didn't fit. Her father must have been alive at that point. The lightskimmer hadn't stopped because he was dead. It had stopped because it had been ordered to.

It had stopped...

There was nothing remarkable about the place where she now was. Perhaps, three months before, it would have lain on a nexus of the electromagnetic field, but the currents had changed since then.

There was silence around her. No crackles from her closed communication channel, no more noise from the aurora. Ruth was about to call the map of the magnetic field when a burst of noise through her implants made her pause.

There was no place the noise could have come from.

Unless...

She lay in her lightskimmer, and waited.

And they came, gradually, coalescing into existence around her, quivering, half-transparent shapes that caught and reflected the light of the aurora.

Ghosts.

Her father had found the meeting place of a herd of Ghosts.

They were crowding around her now, nudging her lightskimmer. She could see through their organs, pulsing through the jelly of their bodies, and somehow it wasn't frightening or ridiculous.

Light flowed through them, red, then yellow-green. The Ghosts withdrew from her at last, their curiosity no doubt sated. They started to move, slowly, as if to a music only they could hear, pulsing to a rhythm of their own.

Ruth, fascinated, watched them. No one had ever been so close to Ghosts before. No one had witnessed that slow dance within the aurora.

The light was green again, and filled with bands and rays that started to move faster and faster. The electrical field would be going wild by now.

The Ghosts had stopped dancing; they'd gathered in a circle around Ruth. The light flooded their bodies, pulsed within their organs. The wedge-shaped bodies quivered, as if with excitement, and the aliens started to move again, in patterns that were no longer slow or stately, but filled with a strange urgency that gripped Ruth as well, made her long to be part of that incomprehensible dance.

The light around her had changed colour, deepened into blue. The Ghosts' bodies glowed purple now. Ruth couldn't tear her eyes from the spectacle before her. She felt, instinctively, that it was nearing its climax, that she would be there to witness it, to bring that beauty back to Silica, to share it with everyone she met. She'd tell Javier, and he'd be awestruck...

Javier.

Her father's friend.

Her father had died here.

It stopped her. Her ecstasy faded, gradually replaced by fear. She again stared at the Ghosts clustered around her, emitting purple light.

Purple. The most energetic of all visible frequencies.

The Ghosts weren't only feeding on the aurora's light. They were amplifying it.

Her shield gauge had been flashing red for a while now. She'd been so lost in the sight before her that she hadn't seen it.

Her hands tightened on the handles of the lightskimmer; she gave the command to accelerate. Her shield gauge wasn't flashing any more. She wasn't sure it was a good sign.

Her lightskimmer tore through the assembled Ghosts. She could almost imagine them shrieking their outrage, but of course they had no vocal chords.

And, as she speeded away, desperately hoping she would survive, she understood at last. He'd been so happy that night, her father, so happy that his daughter had taken after him, so deliriously happy that they'd started talking to each other again, that she'd sent him an animation that very morning. So happy. So careless. He hadn't seen the danger.

The lightskimmer started vibrating under her, but it wasn't the motors. The EM shield was caving in.

Damn. How far was she from the aurora's edge? A hundred kilometres at least. She wouldn't have time to reach the end of the zone before the shield collapsed.

Unbidden, her father's flight log flashed in front of her. The slow, lazy arc through the aurora, the long stop while the Ghosts gathered around him. The final plunge into the atmosphere.

The plunge.

That was it. The edge of the auroral zone wasn't a hundred kilometres south of her. It was a bare ten kilometres under her.

Her father must have attempted that, Ruth realized as she forced the nose of her lightskimmer downwards. He must have understood where safety lay. But still he had died.

The altimeter flashed on her field of vision as she drove the lightskimmer into the sharpest dive she thought the craft would bear. A hundred kilometres. Ninety-eight, ninety-six...

Please please, Ruth prayed to the unfeeling lights around her. Don't take both of us.

Ninety-two...

She could feel the edge of the EM field, a tingle on her back and on her nape. She thought of the current that would go through her when it gave in. Several thousands of amperes, Javier had said. Would she feel anything before it killed her?

Ninety-one...

Ninety.

The light around her shifted from green to red, and then was gone. The quivering EM shield held on for the next two kilometres of the descent before it, too, died.

Ruth, shivering, pulled the lightskimmer to a more horizontal position and continued to speed away from the lights. Above her, the aurora was shimmering in all its impersonal glory: the beauty that had caught her father after her mother had driven him out, the beauty that had finally killed him.

I'm sorry, she thought, and discovered, shocked, that she was weeping. Tears streamed down her cheeks, under the oxygen mask. She wept for the father she had never known, that she had never understood; for the man who'd tried, however awkwardly, to account for abandoning her; for Ben Elemanis, who had spent his life running away from his wife's domineering shadow, and who had found beauty in the sky above Silica, a beauty that had been his funeral pyre.

She was still weeping as the lightskimmer continued its descent to the surface of Silica. Below, a few riders had gathered, hovering under the auroral zone as if hesitant to go back into it.

She could guess Javier would be among them, angrily waiting for her. She already knew what she would tell him.

I understand him now. You were right. I am my father's daughter; and I am proud to be.

THE BROKEN PATHWAY

Gord Sellar

With eyes narrowed, Mo-Sa listened for the reassuring song of even one little mountain bird.

He heard none.

Without breaking stride, he ran his fingers over his stubbled scalp and looked up into the sky. Above, the gnarled black branches of the trees reached upward, naked under a grey and cloudy heaven. He wondered to himself whether the *san-shin* — the local mountain-god — was teasing with him by hiding the path. He caught the vague scent of the coming snow on a gentle wind that passed among the trees, the same insistent wind that chilled him through his thinly padded monk's coat.

Winter had come to the Kingdom of Chosŏn. The only sound that followed him was the crunch of dead leaves beneath his feet. Mo Sa shivered and inhaled through his nose, and when he exhaled through his mouth, his breath poured forth into the cold mountain air as a cloud of thin steam. He felt the gentle tickle of a cough deep in his chest as he began to hum his way through a prayer-song, worrying his prayer beads in one hand as he did so.

He was searching for the fork in the path, the one by the great gnarled grandfather pine. The place where the pathway seemed to branch off almost suddenly, and from which, if one squinted and looked through the trees, one could always glimpse smoke rising in the distance, even on the hottest of mid-summer days.

But winter had transformed the footpath. The last time he'd come, months before, this place had been a den of humid green lushness: creeper vines hanging from the trees, the air heavy with the rolling cascades of the endless song of the *maèmi* — the great rasping choirs of brown cicadas in the branches overhead. Birds, squirrels, mosquitoes, fat bees and careless flies had scurried and

73

buzzed everywhere. As he searched for the missing bend in the path, Mo-Sa was haunted by the scent of peaches that all summer long wafted up from the orchards that sprawled at the foot of the mountain.

Now, only the pines were green. All around him lay the dead hues of fallen leaves, strands of desiccated vines, and fallen logs bared like bones to heaven. Drab brown mud spread out everywhere as though in mourning for the death of another year. It was as if the life had gone out of the land, and as if a little had gone out of Mo-Sa himself. And worse, as he gazed around, he could not find the twist in the path that he remembered, the turn that led down the mountain to Boksagol, the Peach Village, below. He peered anxiously about, wondering whether the *san-shin* — the spirit of the mountain — was having fun with him.

That was when a thin brown cat — a scraggly little thing — scurried across the path. It stopped just off the muddy footpath, staring at him intently, not a bit frightened.

"Hey, Nabi," he called out to it. *Butterfly*, it meant, a common name for kittens. The cat just stared at him, and then, slowly, turned and took a few steps off into the brush. It stopped again, turning and looking at him as if to inquire why he was not following.

"What is it?" he asked. "I have no food for you, Nabi," he muttered.

The cat meowed and stood there. Staring. Waiting.

"Why?" he asked, and started after the kitten. It responded by scurrying off into the brush, not too quickly or too far, and Mo-Sa trailed behind it, as he had done to other cats around the monastery during his childhood.

Beyond a few old, dead trees, he found the cat meowing again loudly and scratching itself against something sticking out of the ground.

"What is it?" he asked the cat. It simply meowed back at him, and stepped back as he came closer to reveal some kind of iron spike that had been driven straight into the stone. Mo-Sa squatted and peered at it, brushing with with one hand to remove the few strands of cat-hair that clung there. It bore no rust, which meant it had not been exposed to the later summer rains. It had been driven in sometime during the autumn. Around the base of the spike, the smallest particles of stone remained in their original cracks.

Inscriptions ran along its side. Some of the characters he recognized — they were the same ones used in Chosŏn, taken from the Middle Kingdom — but interspersed with these was some other, strange kind of writing. He could not read it, but he knew enough to recognize it. *Wae*, he thought, and dread emanated through him. The *Wae* — had they crossed the Eastern Sea in their steam-powered warships, to drive spikes into mountains? Had their warmongering emperor, Mutsuhito, gone mad? Could they be such fools as that?

"What is this, Nabi?" he asked, and the cat just stared up at him, silent now. The cat's stare was pointed, too intense to not mean something.

As he made his way back to the path, he paused by a low-hanging branch and, with a small bit of cloth from his pack, he tied a marker on the branch before continuing down the footpath.

Suddenly, his route seemed clear: *"At'da!"* he said, smiling, with a clap of his hands. Just a little further on, the grandfather pine was visible. Mo-Sa squinted and saw the fuzzy column of smoke rising up. He was near Boksagol after all.

Mo-Sa's step was lighter again as he made his way down the trail. An old stoop-backed man with a cane, dressed in a granite-coloured overcoat, was coming up the trail as Mo-Sa passed him, and looked up into his face. The old fellow's thin white beard hung long from his chin, and his moustaches flowed down from his face like frothy water over a rocky mountain cliff.

Mo-Sa bowed his head respectfully, clasping his hands together as he did so, but the old man's gaze had pushed past the monk without a moment's pause. Mo-Sa didn't mind; the fellow seemed too old to care for the politeness of total strangers, let alone wandering monks.

As he hurried down the hillside, the scent of smoke suddenly tingled in his nose, and thickened. Mo-Sa smiled. He would arrive soon, before the snow began falling.

*

The floor was wonderfully hot. Doubtless a slave or servant somewhere was kept busy constantly stoking the embers, and keeping vigilant guard against any unfortunate conflagration.

Yet for all the luxury of his home, Gentleman Scholar Kwon's body was stiff with tension. He seemed to bear the stresses of the whole province in his back, and its mountains' weight upon his shoulders. Everyone was tense, of course. The rebel peasants to the south had brought trouble upon the whole kingdom. But Kwon's body was actually stiff with the pain. Mo-Sa shook his head and let out a dubious sigh.

"Perhaps a physician could better help you?" he suggested, politely.

"No, no. Those bastards only want to sell me powdered tiger's fang, the ash of burnt phoenix feather, bear's gall bladder, and whale flesh. Charlatans, those physicians. You monks, you're the ones who understand *gi* flows, how the pathways get broken."

"Alright," Mo-Sa said. "Please breathe deeply and hold your breath inside." Gentleman Scholar Kwon obeyed, and onto the man's back, Mo-Sa set his fingertips. Closing his eyes and pressing gently, the monk imagined his fingertips extending into the muscle, where they could touch the *gi* flows directly. The sensation followed suddenly: his fingers being bathed in luminous, warm flows. He searched for the weakest pathways, and followed them along the man's spine, up to a cool darkness buried beneath the bone.

Gentleman Scholar Kwon exhaled.

"Aha," Mo-Sa said. "Beneath your shoulder-blades. Like a bird with its wings snapped. Please, breathe deeply once more..." Mo-Sa rested his hand upon Kwon's shoulder-blade, and as he inhaled, the monk pressed bruisingly hard with his fingertips and thumb for one moment, ignoring the strange stiffness in his own hands. The sensation of blocked, frustrated energy was much stronger there. "This is the strained *hyŏl.*"

The gentleman only grunted.

Mo-Sa drew a small case from the pack that lay nearby and opened it. Within, a set of dozens of miniature needles gleamed.

"All of the *hyŏl* are important. But this *hyŏl* under your shoulder-blade which is blocked now, it is a very important one. It is a great *hyŏl*, an important nexus for the energies that flow throughout your body. It regulates several other such *hyŏl*, and controls the flow of *gi* to your heart, your brain, your liver. We need to restore free flow in this energy centre."

Once more, the gentleman only grunted, and Mo-Sa set out to work. His needles were thin and very sharp, so that very little blood came from where he inserted them, and only twice did the gentleman stiffen from pain. Needle after needle pierced the scholar's flesh, and every once in a while Mo-Sa paused to touch his fingers to the bare skin of the man's back to try gauge the changes in flow. He built careful patterns with the needles, sometimes easing the *gi* flow down a channel between two *hyŏl*, and sometimes blocking a flow so that the *gi* was redirected back to a blocked *hyŏl*, to ease it open.

"Alright," he said softly. "Now stay still, try to breathe deeply, and relax." Sitting back from the man, he softly shut the needle-case and put it away, picking at the loose cat hairs on the floor that seemed to have fallen from his trousers and carefully replacing them inside his pack as well.

Though he could not see outside, he guessed that snow had begun to descend by then. It would be a difficult walk home. Mo-Sa sat down with his legs crossed under him, paying no attention to the unusual ache that passed through them, and closed his eyes for just a moment. The one thing a monk can always do is wait.

When he turned his eyes again to the needles standing up from his patient's back, Mo-Sa's mind turned immediately back to the iron spike he'd found hammered into the mountain stone. He shivered suddenly as he realized the thing's dark purpose.

*

Snow drifted down in wide, bright flakes. Already it blanketed the ground almost completely, and trees nearby balanced stacks of it on their branches. A slight breeze from the west made the falling flakes dance and swirl eastward.

Mo-Sa walked as quickly as he could, staring at anything to distract himself from his panic. As he reached the foot of Wonmi Mountain, the monk chided himself for his fascination with Kwon's wealth. Gentleman Scholar Kwon's home was lavish, and Mo-Sa envied his comforts. He knew he shouldn't, but he did. How many people in the world lived in such luxury? Different tables for food and for writing, and yet another for tea? Such fine ceramic for the tea cups, and such fine, expensive tea as well! The flavour of that wondrous tea lingered in Mo-Sa's mouth still.

And yet, he thought to himself with practised sincerity, none of that averts the inevitable. Death, and then another life, and another. And those dark thoughts brought him back to the iron spike. The *Wae* spike in the mountain's flesh.

The trail was treacherously slippery with new snow. On the way down, he'd been able to see the snags of root and outcroppings of stone, so that almost every footstep had been secure and solid. Now, picking his way along, each footstep began as a test of how lightly he could step, of whether the ground would hold beneath him.

He almost missed the marker he'd left behind — the small white band of cloth tied upon the branch was half-covered in snow — but when he found it, he had to fight himself not to stop and look again at the horrid thing. But he did not have to look at it to know what the spike was; he was certain of it. His heart thudded, and he shivered just as the monastery's gong rang out across the mountainside, calling the monks to evening prayers. He was closer to home than he'd thought.

As the sun sank down and shadows began to grasp at the trees and bushes along the spine of the mountain, Mo-Sa began to run as hard as he could.

*

"Sakamŭni," the monks prayed, led by Senior Monk Hwang "Oh, Sakamŭni." Off to the side, a young monk beat the great drum as the others chanted: *"Namuuu … amiiii … taaaa … bul…"* Their hymn was sullied by coughs and sniffles and cleared throats. Never before had so many monks taken ill at once. Mo-Sa removed his slippers and hurried into the Main Buddha Hall with his head bent low, his face penitent. He knelt with a groan and joined in on the chant, but his mind kept turning back to that iron spike, and a sour horror curdled in his belly as he thought of it.

Now he was sure, the *san-shin* — the god of Wonmi Mountain — had led him off the pathway for a reason. He could feel the energy disruption in the mountain beneath him, just as he'd felt the disturbances in the *hyŏl* of Gentleman Scholar Kwon's back. The *gi* blockage had even spread into Mo-Sa's body. As he genuflected, head to floor, before the statues and paintings of the Buddha, he felt himself on the verge of collapsing.

*

"An iron spike?" Hwang Ryu said, the crow's feet at the edge of his eyes flexing. He sniffled his runny nose and squinted.

"Yes, Respected Elder Monk, sir. An iron spike. Driven into the stone of the mountain."

"Why?"

"I think…" Mo-Sa breathed deeply, and shivered in horror. "I think it is an attack on the San Shin. In Sosa, I performed acupuncture on Gentleman Scholar Kwon, and I realized…"

"Ah," the elderly monk said, sniffling as he nodded. "Geomantic attack. But … who?" he asked, clearing his throat noisily in disgust.

"The spike is engraved with foreign words."

Old Hwang Ryu looked out of the door of his sleeping chamber, into the starry, moonless dark of the early night. "Foreign geomancers?" he asked, raising his hand to his white-stubbled crown, and scratching at the shadows that the lamplight cast upon his scalp.

"*Wae* sorcerers," Mo-Sa said, and the old man stared at him in silence for a long time.

"Tomorrow," Hwang Ryu finally said. "You will show us."

*

The morning came late, heavy and chill, and Mo-Sa woke slowly from a dream that he could not remember, but which would haunt him as he washed his face and ate a little rice and salty soup with the other monks. The dream haunted him like the last bird of autumn, soaring across the sky to the south. The black speck of the bird flying away remained barely visible in the distance, impossible to see but also impossible to forget.

With each step, he sank his foot into the snow. In places, it was deep enough to cover his whole ankle. A hand's breadth and a half, perhaps more, had fallen during the night. Elder Monk Hwang Ryu's coughing reminded him to slow his pace, and he blinked his eyes against the whiteness.

After an hour's slow and sickly hiking, he finally sighted the marker that he'd tied around the tree branch the night before.

"Here it is! Over here," he said, and led the shivering, sneezing monks past the marked branch, cautioning them politely to be very careful. Nudging past a frozen, leafless bush, he stepped out of the trees to the bare piece of rock where he'd found the stake. It was still there, half-hidden by snow. The soles of his slippers flat to the ground, Mo-Sa squatted and brushed the deep snow away from the spike with his bare hands, finally wiping the remaining snow from the spike itself.

Hwang Ryu squatted beside him, squinting at the text stamped into the iron, and slowly, still squatting, made his way around the stake, to the side where the sun shone directly on it.

"It is *Wae*," he said, nodding. The old monk glanced nervously at the two brothers who'd accompanied him and Mo-Sa to the spike, and then at Mo-Sa himself. "They're here."

They all stared at the spike for a moment, a silence full of fear and worry and anger and shame blooming between them in the cold, wintry air. A young monk coughed, a brutal hack that took hold of his whole body, and Senior Monk Hwang turned and stared at the boy, his eyes anxious.

Mo-Sa realized what Hwang must already have understood. The sickness that had struck monastery and town alike this year — it had been too sudden, too intense. The failed crop of the fall before. If there were more spikes...

Hwang Ryu was the first to speak: "Tae Gui," he said to the one of the two brothers still standing. "There must be others. Go get the other brothers. We need to find every last spike on this mountain." Turning to the other monk, Mi Reu, a young, powerful-bodied boy of fifteen, he said, "We must send word to Bongeun Temple. Go, run, fast as you can, all the way to Hanyang," the monk said. The capital: it was a long walk. Running all day long, he would be lucky to reach the monastery sometime well after sunset — assuming he could find a boat to ferry him across at Mapo port that late in the day. "Borrow a horse from the village if you can. They must send word out to all the mountain monasteries to search. This is an emergency of the highest order." The monks nodded and hurried away in the direction of the monastery, struggling against their weakened state.

Hwang Ryu clucked his tongue and lamented, *"Aigo."* Mo-Sa rarely heard him say the word, so plaintive and regretful it was. "The *Wae*. I had heard they had wicked plans, but…"

"Respected Elder Hwang," Mo-Sa said, "I tried last night, but I could not feel the gi flow in the mountain. I know how to find the *hyŏl* in a man's body, but in a mountain's… I don't know where to begin."

The old monk nodded. "Nor do I. The last monk in our temple who knew that sort of thing died of old age before you were even born. We shall need expert help, but first, we must find the other spikes. A single spike is not a conspiracy, just an annoyance."

"Shall we begin the search now, Elder Monk, sir?" Mo-Sa asked, rising and extending his hand to help Hwang Ryu rise.

"No," the old monk said, chuckling as he took the young monk's hand and pulled himself up. "These other boys can organize that. You and I will go see Gentleman Scholar Kwon," he explained, with a nod toward Sosa. *"He* will know if there have been any *Wae* poking about." With that, the old man set out towards the trail that led to the Peach Village below, all blanketed in snow.

*

The mild scent of tea wafted from the pot, borne on the steam, and Mo-Sa watched Kwon's daughter intently as she set the lid down on the teapot.

"Wae?" Kwon spat the word out with disdain, and cleared his raspy throat. Like most of his countrymen, he had no love of the people from the island empire across the Eastern Sea, traders and pirates alike. "Yes, there is one of those dogs in town. He arrived a few weeks ago. He has a woman with him, sixteen years old perhaps. A girl from our country. Talks as if she wasn't born a peasant. He told me she was his wife when he arrived. He has a charter from the king, so we set him up in an ambassadorial residence." He wiped his nose.

"Our king?" Hwang Ryu asked, glancing at the teapot. Kwon's daughter picked it up and poured the harsh first brewing of tea out into a waste-water bowl. Daintily lifting the lid, she added more hot water to the leaves in the pot.

"Yes," Gentleman Scholar Kwon said with a frown. "There are too many damned *Wae* in the capital. The poor king is beset by them. There's more of them hanging around the palace than there are rats, ever since the peasants began rebelling down south, and the *Wae* are always demanding something from him. It doesn't seem enough to them that they are defeating the Middle Kingdom in this ridiculous war of theirs. Their damned emperor wants to stick his spoon into every soup bowl in the world."

"And this *Wae* who came to town, is he still here?"

"I imagine so, but it's hard to catch him. Half the time he's wandering around with a sketch-pad, and the rest of the time he's carrying equipment out into the woods and doesn't come back until dark," Kwon said, adjusting his scholar's hat, and nudging his daughter.

She began to pour tea into the small teacups, setting one before the elderly monk first, then her father, and finally before Mo-Sa. They all took the cups at the same time, but Mo-Sa waited until they both had tasted tea before he sipped his. He sighed softly, inhaling the warm steam, savouring the scent of the tea.

"Equipment?" Hwang Ryu asked, taking a mouthful of the tea.

"Yes," Kwon nodded, sipping. "A satchel full of equipment. And spikes, like the ones you describe. He has a pony to carry it all."

Mo-Sa drank his tea quickly, cringing as it burned his mouth. Then he set the cup on the table.

"We should go to his residence," Hwang said in a firm, hard voice. "Have a look."

"Of course," Kwon said. "Daughter," he called, and the girl looked up at him. "Pour these good monks one last cup of hot tea before we go."

They all placed their cups on the table, and all of them watched as the girl poured the tea into one cup after another. Hwang and Kwon swallowed their tea quickly. Neither of them noticed when Mo-Sa, merely sipping, placed the cup down still half-full. Only Kwon's daughter saw it, and looked up at him as if to find what it meant on his face. By the darkness under her eyes, Mo-Sa could guess that she, too, was ill and sleeping poorly.

"Let's go," the old monk said, and the other men quickly rose to their feet.

*

"Why, what are you doing?" she screamed.

Can this girl really be anyone's wife? Mo-Sa asked himself, standing barefoot on the hot floor of the house. The faint smell of smoke filled the air. The girl was so skinny, she looked as if she hadn't eaten in a week, and she thrashed her arms about as she yelled.

"Have you lost your mind, girl?" Hwang said, and Kwon nodded to one of the servants he'd brought along, a man dressed up as an official precinct guardsman. The servant picked the girl up and hauled her outside, while Mo-Sa and Kwon looked around the room.

Mo-Sa quickly found a sheaf of papers, with what looked like strange maps of the area, the city a tiny spot and the mountains networked with lines that looked like veins flowing with blood. *Gi flows,* Mo-Sa thought, and he spotted strange markings along these lines that suggested, perhaps, even *hyŏl*. The words on the map were mostly in the *Wae* language however, without even a few of the old Chinese characters for him to guess at.

"Sir!" Mo-Sa said. He began to cough as Hwang stepped forward to take the map from him. Staring at it, the old monk wore only a puzzled look.

"Perhaps he *is* a mapmaker," Kwon said, shrugging.

Hwang shook his head. "This map … it is too strange. The way he draws the mountains…" The monk pointed at the map, where the mountains were drawn to look like pools of water, their surfaces ripping as if from thrown stones.

"Yes," Mo-Sa said. "It looks like he is mapping the *gi* of the land." The woman was still yelling outside; he could hear her through the open door.

"Why?" Kwon asked. "For what purpose?"

Hwang gritted his teeth. "We build monasteries on mountainsides for a reason: the strength of our land flows through the mountains. Our palaces and capitals have always been placed between mountains to the north and rivers to the south. The energy that gathers in those places, it is the lifeblood of Chosŏn."

Hwang rolled up the map as Kwon and Mo-Sa watched. "If he can kill the spirits of the mountains, then the strength of our country will soon follow. We must get the girl to tell us where he has gone."

*

Sullen-faced, the wild-eyed Chosŏn girl marched through the snow, wrapped in blankets and wearing a pair of woven-straw shoes that were a little too big for her feet. Behind her, silently, the monks, Gentleman Scholar Kwon and several local guardsmen all followed, tromping through the snow toward the barren peach orchard where branches reached up bare and desperate towards heaven. As they passed, villagers paused at their work to stare. Women stopped toiling at their outdoor cookfires and called their husbands; maids lifted their wooden paddles and stopped thumping freshly-washed linens flat, watching through clouds of their misty breath. Children followed at some distance, calling out to one another, laughing and chattering. Old women and men gathered together inside a tea shop came outside to watch the crowd pass.

Halfway across the orchard though, the spectacle had died away, and only a few children trailed behind. Kwon and Hwang ignored them, but Mo-Sa couldn't help but look at them. They made him think of when he was young, of his orphan days when he had run gleefully among the trees at the temple, chasing sparrows and shrieking at turtles, diving after fish in a stream at the foot of the mountain.

By the time they'd crossed the orchard and drawn close to the mountain beyond, the crowd had dwindled down to a few children following solemnly, poking one another and whispering occasionally. Mo-Sa turned once in a while to give them an imperious look, but when he did they either froze in place, heads bowed and penitent, or ducked behind the bare-branched peach trees and hid, giggling.

The woman began calling out: *"Tōru! Tōru!"* Her screeching voice echoed back down from the walls of the mountain and she stared up into the snow-covered forest of pines and black leafless branches. *"Tōru!"* she shouted once more, and closed her eyes to listen.

A voice called out from somewhere high above.

She replied with a string of foreign words. Mo-Sa stared at her as if he'd just seen a talking rabbit, and wondered if the *Wae* man had ever borne this woman back across the Eastern Sea to his island homeland.

A voice replied, barely audible to Mo-Sa, but she listened with her eyes closed and one hand behind her ear. When the shouting stopped, she turned and faced the men and told them, "He says he is coming now. He is very high up. It will take time."

"No," Hwang Ryu said, shaking his fist. "He may hide his spikes, his maps, and ready his weapons and traps. We must find him now. You, little wife, shut your mouth."

But she quickly said, "Weapons? He has no weapons! He is a scholar, like this man!" She nodded towards Kwon.

"Quiet," Mo-Sa hissed at her.

The girl began immediately to holler in the foreigner's language, but she only got a few phrases out before Mo-Sa managed to grab her and she burst into a shrill scream. A guard took her from him and clapped a hand over her mouth, muffling her voice. She struggled, but he held her firm.

The distant voice above called out, once, and then again, and went silent.

"Let's go," old Hwang said, and with spry footsteps he picked his way up the side of the mountain, leading the group toward the stranger above.

*

The man came crashing down the trail so quickly that he almost ran straight into Senior Monk Hwang.

He didn't look like a *Wae*, not like in the stories Mo-Sa had heard all his life. The monk had grown up with the impression that the *Wae* were monstrous, murderous sea bandits and a lower order of life than human, perhaps on the same level as bush goblins and devils. But this fellow looked just like a man of about forty, the sort of man one might see passing through the village on his way from Chemulpo to the capital, Hanyang.

He was tall, taller than Mo-Sa, and wore the same strange western-styled clothing that city men sometimes wore: pantaloons the colour of tilled earth, with a curious crease down the front, and small black leather shoes coated in snow, and a thick jacket with a hood. On his moustachioed face, the man wore a set of small, round-rimmed spectacles, which gave him an odd, sophisticated appearance. His hair was slicked back as if he'd recently showered, and there were hints of grey at his temples.

The fellow rushed toward the group empty-handed, jabbering in half-comprehensible Korean that he had to pass, excuse him, he had to go, until he caught a glimpse of the girl in one of the guard's clutches. The other guardsmen stepped forward and grabbed him by the arms.

"Why?" he yelled, and then began jabbering in his own language. "Why? My wife!" he cried again, but the guards ignored his words. Somehow the man's wife managed to wriggle her head free and she began to holler at the *Wae* too, in his language, until the guardsman shut her up again. She struggled with

82

a fierceness that shocked Mo-Sa.

"Take him to my home, tie him up and watch him carefully," Kwon said to the guardsmen who had the man. "And you," he told the man holding the wriggling girl, "bring her up the mountain with us. Better to keep them separated."

The guard nodded, and once again they resumed their climb up the mountainside, with the elderly monk at the lead.

*

They found the end of the trail of footprints only when the sun had become a bright red ember, setting already. Scattered on the ground were a few sheets of paper and writing instruments, a compass, some strange metal tools, and a satchel of long iron stakes beside a heavy, iron-headed mallet.

"Let's see," said Mo-Sa, sliding one of the spikes out of the bag and holding it up for Hwang to inspect.

The old man peered at the stake for a few moments before nodding. "The same!" the old man yelped, and made a fist, looking around. But his eyes narrowed and his jaw trembled as his gaze settled on a spot a little distance off.

Mo-Sa followed the old man's gaze and, after a moment, he saw it too: a small area cleared of snow, and a rusty iron spike sticking up out of the stone beneath.

They hurried over, Hwang Ryu and Kwon bending down to look at the spike. That was all there was room for, so Mo-Sa stood back, trying to ignore the girl's eyes on him. When she didn't turn her gaze from him, he turned and stared at her for a moment, but her eyes were too hard, too angry to bear looking at. He finally averted his gaze, staring at the bare-branched trees all around.

Then he noticed it.

"*What?* Look ... the trees..." Mo-Sa mumbled, pointing all around. Hwang and Kwon rose up and followed the young monk's gaze, and after a moment their eyes widened. Every pine within fifty paces of the spike was dead. A few bore crests of orange needles, the normal colour for dead mountain pine, but the needles on many others were night-black and hung long and ominous, like the hair on a widowed maiden, nearly brushing the snowy ground.

*

"What is this?" Kwon hollered at the foreign man, who was tied up and sitting on the floor inside Kwon's home, his coat and shoes removed. He was wearing a Western-styled shirt and tie, and even socks, and he could have easily passed for a dignitary from the capital, except for the blood that dribbled from his nose onto his white shirt and his fancy crease-fronted trousers.

"...spike ... map..." the man said. Those were the only recognizable words amid a flurry of garbled, heavily-accented speech. His wife stared at Kwon angrily, but she began to translate for him.

"He says it's a spike that he uses to measure the height of mountains. The spikes show him how tall mountains are at different spots and he uses it in his maps."

Hwang sighed angrily, disgusted by the story. The man had definitely planned this alibi, for he had several half-drawn maps in among his things.

"Ask him who sent him."

She didn't bother. She didn't have to ask. "The Great Emperor Mutsuhito of the Great Empire of Nippon..."

"Aie," Kwon hissed. "Great Empire?"

"Dog Empire," Mo-Sa spat out angrily. "How can you speak of the the *Wae* that way? After all the trouble they have caused our kingdom?"

She pursed her lips together, ready to cry, as if some untold story were fighting to be spoken. The stranger suddenly asked her a question. She spoke, and he replied quickly and harshly. Tears in her eyes, she said, "He was sent to map the land from here to the Western coast. Nippon and the Middle Kingdom are at war..."

The man interrupted her again.

"...and he wants to know why you're interfering with his business. He says it's harmless." She caught Mo-Sa's eye, and immediately looked down into her lap. She was hiding something.

"Tell him we want to know where he bought you," Kwon said, his eyes narrowed.

"No," she said.

"What?! You *insolent*..."

"No, I mean, he didn't *buy* me, sir. He saved my life. I'm an orphan and ... he's the first person who ever helped me."

"Lies!" Kwon shouted. "Tell him we know what the spikes are for! Tell him we know exactly what he's doing and..."

Mo-Sa stared at the young woman and he knew that she was telling the truth, and that she was hiding something. But she was, definitely, an orphan. One homeless pup knows another by its bark. The foreigner *had* taken her in, and helped her, and perhaps even really married her.

But that didn't mean he wasn't also waging war on Chosŏn.

"Tell him we know what the spikes are," Kwon said. "That we know what he is trying to do, to break the flow of *gi* in our mountains. To weaken and destroy our nation so that the *Wae* can invade again, as they did in the time of King Sŏnjo."

She stared at them for a moment, and then said with a shake of her head, "I don't know how to say all that in his language."

Kwon cursed and slapped the girl, and inwardly Mo-Sa cringed. Just then, a knock came at the door. Kwon's daughter opened it and, in the darkness outside, a pair of young monks from the temple stood shivering, terror on their faces.

Kwon and Hwang went outside, and Mo-Sa followed them. He could only hear a little bit of what the younger monks were saying, but he caught enough to feel a horrible clenching in the pit of his stomach. Dozens of spikes had been found, all over Wonmi mountain, and some of the monks who'd run to nearby mountains had come back with word of more findings. Signal fires, they said, were burning all across the country, and the capital was in an uproar.

"We must *kill* him," Kwon said, with a soft voice but with a chilling certainty. He had said it loudly enough for Mo-Sa to hear, though he did not turn his gaze from the elder monk before him.

Hwang turned and looked at Mo-Sa, whose face showed both shock and opposition to the action. Hwang's rheumy eyes were hard with anger, but Mo-Sa suspected that the old monk might not allow such an execution.

The younger monk braced himself quickly and approached the two men. "Respected Gentleman Scholar Kwon," he said, bowing his head briefly so as to show respect, but then looking the scholar in the eye. "Of course I am not a government officer, and far be it from me to tell you how to rule, but a suggestion, perhaps…"

"You would aid the enemy of our kingdom?" Kwon cleared his throat, folding his hands together behind his back as if preparing to remonstrate the young, upstart monk. "He's lying. Surely you don't believe he knows nothing of geomancy?"

Mo-Sa gazed into the scholar's face, wondering just how much *he* knew about geomancy. "No, sir. On the contrary. I fear perhaps he knows more than we imagined. Enough to find the *hyŏl* of a mountain and cripple it. To kill the spirit of a mountain even," he said, thinking of the *san-shin* who, disguised as a cat, had led him to the spike on Wonmi Mountain. "But if he knows this sort of thing … perhaps we should make him teach us? Perhaps *we* will need to know how to do this too. To undo what he has done. And … there *are* mountains on their islands too, sir. In the *Wae* homeland."

He braced himself for Kwon's response. If it was negative, he would have saved a little face for Hwang. But Kwon's response surprised him. "Yes, yes," he said. "Of course. That is a very good idea. Clever thinking," he grumbled with a stern nod.

Mo-Sa glanced at Hwang, preparing himself to apologize for speaking out of turn, or to credit Hwang with the idea, but the old fellow's eyes were smiling as he turned to Kwon and nodded.

"Shall we go inside?" Kwon said, ending his question with a rasping cough. "We can sip tea and think this over. But don't let on that we don't plan to kill him," the scholar admonished Mo-Sa, in the most sage voice he could muster. "A scared man will confess more than one who knows he will survive the night."

"Yes, sir," Mo-Sa said, nodding and catching Hwang's eye. They followed the scholar inside, trying not to look sleepy.

The foreigner sat there, still, arms bound behind his back.

"Servant!" Kwon called out impatiently. When the skinny young fellow appeared, he said, "Tie up his legs and carry him into another room. I'm tired of seeing his face tonight, and I want a break before we torture him." When the girl reacted, he said, "Throw his woman in with him. I'm tired of her too."

*

"What are we going to do?" Mo-Sa asked Hwang, and the old monk stared off into the darkness.

"Listen," Hwang whispered, and then shut his lips tight.

Mo-Sa closed his eyes and held his breath, and he heard it too. A low, constant sound, like the slow shifting of a mountain in its sleep, or the groan of some distant gargantuan beast out in the darkness. They stood together without speaking, and the faint rumble grew slightly.

"*We* aren't going to do anything," Hwang finally said. "Gentleman Scholar Kwon is a government officer,and we are just monks. What happens now is up to him." He sniffled.

"But … he is listening to our advice. What shall we tell him, sir?"

The old monk sighed and touched his shoulder carefully. "What do you think, Mo-Sa?" he asked.

"I don't know. Map-making … perhaps. Yet why the strange tools?"

"The *Wae* are strange people," Hwang stated with a resigned wobble of his head. "Perhaps they have invented this? A new weapon to attack us with? If we went to their islands, do you think we would find spikes in *their* mountains?"

"Well..." Mo-Sa said. "If they did it right, just like with a human body, it would..."

"Empower them beyond belief," Hwang said, and he went pale. *"Aigo."*

"Yes."

"Especially if they had crippled our *gi*," Hwang remarked. "What we really need is a geomancer. A scholar. Someone from Hanyang. But it will take days before someone like that arrives. I have a feeling that Hwang will want to kill the foreigner before that." The old monk turned to face the direction of Wonmi mountain, but his eyes were on the heavens. Squinting, he said, "Tell me, Mo-Sa, do you see *Hwasŏng?*"

The young monk gazed up into the wide darkness of the sky, searching for the speck of red that he knew the older monk could not see, 'the star of fire'. Finally, he replied, "Yes."

"And *Tosŏng?*" the monk asked.

Mo-Sa searched the sky again, but 'the earth star' was nowhere to be seen. "No," he said after a few moments.

"Mmm," the monk said, rubbing his hands and then cupping them together and blowing his warm breath into them. "We must talk to him. Let us go and see whether we can get Kwon to let us visit this man again. *Alone.*"

Mo-Sa nodded, and glanced off into the darkness, where the low, deep sound continued, still so gentle that it was almost inaudible.

*

The foreigner sat shivering, arms bound behind his back, in an unheated room in the back of Kwon's home, his wife seated on the floor beside him. Mo-Sa had the man's thickly padded coat in his hand and he set out to put it on his shoulders as the man began to babble in *Wae*.

"He says to put it on me," the foreigner's wife said.

Mo-Sa nodded and draped the jacket around the woman's quivering shoulders. Hwang said, "Young woman." She looked into the old monk's eyes, and suddenly she did not look so much a woman as a child — a terrified young thing.

"Your husband," Hwang went on, "is suspected of some terrible crimes." She began to weep, and none of her husband's incomprehensible prattle seemed to stop her. "We need you to help us to talk to him."

"Yes," she said. "But please, don't let them... I don't want ... *please* don't kill him."

Hwang nodded to Mo-Sa, who said, "The map-making. We believe your husband was doing that. That in itself is enough of a crime ... making maps for the *Wae*, to help them invade..."

"You don't understand!" she said, tears rolling down her cheeks. Her husband began to babble to her, and she responded in his language, her words mangled by sobbing.

"...but we believe he is doing more than just making maps," Mo-Sa continued. "We believe the spikes have a function ... that they..." He breathed deeply. "Is your husband a geomancer?"

She was squinting against her tears and sobbing so much that when she spoke, Mo-Sa couldn't understand.

"Don't do this!" the man suddenly cried out in their language, using the most common, informal, rudimentary words possible: "*Hajima! Hajima!*" Over and over again, he begged this way. Hwang held up his hands to silence the man, who cried it out a few more times before stopping. Finally, the monks waited in silence for the woman to stop crying.

"When he found me," she said between sobs, "I was left to die ... on the side of a mountain trail... Bandits." She burst into tears again. "I was on the way to my master's brother's house... Every wife hates a pretty concubine... especially one orphaned from a rich family," she said. "He found me; he treated me ... yes, with *chim*, needles in my flesh. They brought back my strength. I was a girl at the time, fifteen. No father, no mother. I spoke a little of his language then, and he taught me more. He married me, though he knew what had been done to me. He is a good man."

Mo-Sa looked over at the *Wae*, but the man was staring at the wall beside him, ignoring the conversation. He looked like someone who was steeling himself for death.

"He told me he was a mapmaker," she said. "I wondered what the spikes were too, but he told me it was only for measuring the land. The height of mountains, the depths of valleys. But one night, I followed him, into the mountains. What he did ... it was not measuring any mountain's height. Reading ancient words from a little leather-bound book, one hand on the spike, another gesturing strangely ... it was a ritual." She glanced at her impassive husband, and Mo-Sa and Hwang exchanged wide-eyed looks as well.

"I interrupted it, and I asked him what he was doing. And do you know what he showed me?" She paused, looked down to the floor as if seeing something on the ground that they could not see. "A broken spike. He told me he'd driven it into the stone of the mountain a year before, when he'd come mapmaking. That he'd been staking mountains for two years already before he'd met me."

Mo-Sa stared at the woman, horrified. "You stayed with him? You betrayed your country for...?"

"No!" she hissed. "The spike he showed me that night, he'd dug it *out* of the stone. The new spike was to *unblock* the mountain's *gi*. He was trying to *undo* what he'd done before."

"Because of you?"

"I don't know," she said. "Yes, maybe because of me. Or because he realized that it was wrong, and cruel. I think he realized what his people might do to mine if our land was weakened enough."

Hwang looked at Mo-Sa, the doubt clear on his face. Mo-Sa could understand; after all, he'd seen the dead trees around the newly-driven spike. With his own eyes, he'd seen it. Yet he knew that to redirect the flow of *gi*, to free a blocked *hyŏl*, sometimes required a new, temporary blockage.

"It's true!" the woman insisted. "Check his bag of spikes! You will find some rusted and broken in pieces. And his maps! They were all made more than a year ago. He marked everywhere the spikes were and..."

Mo-Sa looked to Hwang, who nodded. "I promise we will look," he said. "But I cannot promise that he will be..."

"Please," she said, sobbing again, and she closed her eyes, leaning against her husband. As Mo-Sa and Hwang stood to leave, the husband watched them with anxious, tired eyes.

*

Kwon was outside, arguing with someone. Mo-Sa moved to look out and check who'd come, but Hwang held him back for a moment, listening.

"It's Lord Yi," the old monk finally said, sighing. "All we need now is local government getting involved." Lord Yi, the local government magistrate, hated Kwon and resented his links to the central government. If Yi learned anything of the accusations against the foreigner, there would be a race to see who could execute him first.

Mo-Sa shook his head and crossed the room to where the prisoner's things had been left for Kwon's inspection, beside his writing desk. Bending down, Mo-Sa saw that Kwon had been annotating the objects in the *Wae*'s possession. Skimming the list, he saw, "Stakes, broken: 3."

"Senior Monk Hwang, sir," he said, digging into the bag of stakes. The jagged edges of the cracked stakes lightly scratched his hand, and he pulled out some of the pieces to show Hwang.

The older monk stared at the rusty, snapped lengths of iron and grabbed up a map.

"Look," he said, pointing with his long middle finger at a couple of red spots on the map. Panic spread across his deeply-wrinkled face. "He's been crossing out *hyŏl*. Mo-Sa ... surely she is lying..."

"What if she isn't? What if those are the old spikes he's crossing out? Who else can undo the harm he has done?"

Hwang looked as if he wanted to disagree, but wasn't sure he could.

"We must get them out of here," Mo-Sa whispered.

Hwang nodded, dubiously. "Until a court geomancer comes, at least. Mo-Sa ... I am too old to run with them. You take them out, get them to the temple..."

Mo-Sa stared at the shut door, listening to Lord Yi argue with Kwon. They didn't sound like they were anywhere near a resolution.

"I have an idea," he said, and he stripped off his padded jacket. "For it to succeed, you need to go and distract them. Talk about *hyŏl*, Indian geomancy or something."

Hwang smiled. "I will talk as long as I can."

Mo-Sa nodded. He'd been lectured by Hwang all his life — he knew the old monk would buy him more than enough time.

*

Out of the back door, Mo-Sa led the couple past the wheezing guard asleep at his post beside the rear gate. Out into the darkness, around the edge of the sleeping, torchlit village. Because the snow had long before stopped falling, he could not lead them straight to the trail, along the shortcut he usually used. Instead, he took them to the street that ran through the middle of town.

"This road will turn into a trail," he said softly. "You must follow it east, that way, up the mountainside."

The man spoke to his wife, who translated to Mo-Sa, "He needs his equipment. The spikes, the mapmaking gear. Without it, he can't..."

Mo-Sa shushed her. "We'll get it later. I want you to follow this trail up, and don't stray from it. No matter what you hear, keep going, and don't turn back. I will come and find you later. *Don't leave the trail*," he said. "Now *go*."

He watched them hurry towards the mountain until they disappeared into darkness. They needed time, so he closed his eyes and counted to one hundred as he paced his way back slowly toward Kwon's house.

Then, taking a deep breath, he yelled: "Hey! You! Stop!" He started running down the road, away from Wonmi Mountain, yelling as loud as he could. As he went, lanterns lit within the houses, and villagers emerged groggily to see what the ruckus was about. After a minute or so of hollering, he stopped, panting hard.

A pack of guards — Kwon's and Yi's all together — rushed up from behind him, faces alarmed. Someone must have gone into the room, seen the missing prisoners, the slashed rope scattered on the ground.

"West!" he yelled, and broke out into a cough. "You must catch them!" he added over their shouts.

The guards nodded and ran off to the West in hot pursuit, hollering for the citizens to awaken and join in the search. Behind them, Lord Yi on his horse galloped hard, trying to catch up. Nobody noticed when the young monk failed to charge after them on foot.

By the time Mo-Sa was a third of the way up the mountainside, the shouts of the villagers had died out into silence. The noise he'd heard in the distance earlier was gone too, but his unease remained.

Suddenly, he heard birds. The silence of the afternoon had left him thinking they had utterly abandoned the mountain, but now it seemed that armies of them sang all at once, filling the darkness with their shrill cries. The branches of trees shook and Mo-Sa glimpsed small black forms — squirrels, he imagined — leaping from tree to tree far above. He was sure he heard the shrieking yowl of a cat somewhere nearby.

Then came a sudden jolt. The ground beneath his feet shivered, groaning loudly, and he was thrown down into the snow, against a tree stump. He rose shakily, but the stony mountain shifted again, pushing him down once more.

He waited, and a third violent shudder passed through stone beneath him.

Minutes later, when he was certain the earth had gone still again, he rose, bewildered and lost in the darkness. Yet there was a sound to guide him: a voice was calling out. Not to him though; it was screaming, wailing in horror.

He hurried toward it, and realized it was the girl's voice. Mo-Sa called out to her, time and time again, but she didn't answer. She couldn't hear him over her own screaming.

When Mo-Sa finally found her, she was crouched beside the body of the *Wae* man. He, too, had fallen to the ground during the violence, but a tree had fallen straight onto him, crushing the life from his body. The tree was an old, dead thing with a blackened trunk and greenery, its crooked limbs drooping dark and sickly, the long, diseased needles spread out from them like the hair of a dead virgin's ghost.

"Why?" the girl cried out.

Mo-Sa squatted beside her, searching the darkness for the iron spike he was sure was somewhere nearby, and put his hand on her shoulder. There were many things he did not say to her.

He did not ask her what she would do now, with her man gone, or whether she had a home to return to. He did not ask her name, or her clan, or the name of her home town.

He did not ask her how he and his fellows would know which spikes to pull from the stone, and which, therapeutically, should stay. He asked nothing at all about how his brother monks would even find them all.

He did not speak of the *san-shin*, or justice, or vengeance, or even hope. He said nothing of what might become of her if the king asked to see her. He only put his hand on her shoulder and let the mountaintop silence remain unbroken all around them, while she wept her hot tears into the snow for her dead *Wae* lover.

BIRD-DROPPING AND SUNDAY

Eric James Stone

Merklas the Glass Giant holds the Sun on his shoulder as he paces from East to West across the earth. Does the heat of the Sun singe his fingers? Do his giant feet crush houses and trees beneath them with each hundred-mile step? Will he ever get a day to rest from his labours? These are all good questions, my child, and if you have patience they will all be answered.

But not today. For this is not the tale of Merklas the Glass Giant.

There once was a woman who lived in the left shoe of Merklas. (And she may live there to this day, if she is not dead.) Like the giant himself, the shoe was made of glass so clear you could see right through it and not know anything was there. If the glass was clean, that is. That was the job of the woman: to clean the giant's left shoe. Keeping the whole shoe free from dirt was more work than she could handle alone, but she had seven children of her own to help her. Their names were Sunday, Monday, Tuesday, Wednesday, Thursday, Friday and Saturday.

The woman also had one child not her own. One day an eagle stole a baby boy from his crib. As the bird returned to its nest with its prize, it flew headlong into the left knee of Merklas. The baby fell from the eagle's claws and landed in a glass bucket of soapy water that the woman was using as she cleaned. She fished him out by his ankles and decided to keep him. So she took him into her little glass house inside the arch support of the glass shoe, wrapped him in a glass blanket, and placed him in a glass bed.

With seven children of her own, why did the woman decide to keep the baby? Where was her husband? What did she think about everyone being able to see through the glass into her home? These are all good questions, my child, and if you have patience they will all be answered.

But not today. For this is not the tale of the woman who lived in the giant glass shoe.

It is the tale of the foundling boy.

Since there were no days left to use in naming the boy, the woman did not know how to name him. Finally, because he had been dropped by a bird, she called the boy Bird-Dropping.

Despite his name, Bird-Dropping was a clean boy. A very clean boy. The cleanest boy there ever was before or has been since. No dirt would stick to him. If you dipped him head-down in a barrel of mud he'd come out cleaner than most children come out from being scrubbed in a hot-water bath.

Did he hate the name Bird-Dropping? Could his clothes get dirty? Why would anyone have a barrel full of mud? These are all good questions, my child, and if you have patience they will all be answered.

Of all Bird-Dropping's adopted brothers and sisters, only one treated him kindly. Brother Monday said he was dumb. Sister Tuesday said he was ugly. Brother Wednesday twisted his arm. Sister Thursday pulled his hair. Brother Friday broke his toys. And sister Saturday spit on his breakfast.

But his oldest sister, Sunday, said he was handsome and she told him he was smart. She combed his hair and hugged him, shared her breakfast and fixed his toys. And she told him stories of bold princesses and beautiful warriors — or perhaps it was the other way round.

One day when Bird-Dropping was five years old, the giant's left foot came down near a cave. Since the giant's strides were so long, each foot stayed on the ground for several minutes before the next step. That was long enough that the band of forty thieves who lived in the cave came out to find what had made the noise. When the one-eyed chief of the thieves saw Sunday scrubbing mud from atop the toe of the giant's shoe, he decided to steal her away to be his wife. So he had his thieves surround her, place a sack over her head and carry her back to their cave.

Bird-Dropping heard Sunday's screams and jumped off the shoe to run after her.

At the mouth of the cave, Bird-Dropping tried to sneak in but was caught by one of the thieves, who took him to the chief.

"What are you doing here, little boy?" The chief scowled, making his eye bulge out and the flesh around his empty eye-socket twitch. The scars on his face turned red.

"I'm not just a little boy," said Bird-Dropping, trying to be brave and clever like the princesses in the stories Sunday had told him. "I'm a prince. And my father the king is very angry that you have stolen my sister, the princess. He sent me to tell you to let her go."

The chief of the thieves roared with laughter. All the rest of the thieves laughed too. Their eyes glittered darkly in the firelight.

"Tell me, little boy," said the chief, "why should I believe you are a prince?"

Next to the chief was a barrel of black mud, which was used by the thieves

92

to darken their faces when they went prowling in the night.

"Dip me in that barrel of mud, and you will have proof," said Bird-Dropping.

So the chief of the thieves ordered two of his men to dunk Bird-Dropping head-down into the barrel of mud. And they held him that way for five minutes, until the chief of the thieves was sure the boy must be dead.

But because Bird-Dropping was such a clean boy, the mud couldn't touch him. It left a pocket of air all around him so he could breathe.

When the two thieves hauled Bird-Dropping out of the barrel, everyone was amazed to see that not only was he not dead, but he had not a speck of mud on him, not even on his clothes.

"Only a prince could be of such nobility that not even mud will touch him," said Bird-Dropping.

The chief frowned. "If you're a prince and she's a princess, why do you not dress in fine silks?"

"I can explain," said Sunday, playing along with Bird-Dropping's ruse. "My father the king has us go out among the common folk so that we will understand their needs and be better rulers."

"If you are indeed who you claim to be," said the chief, "why shouldn't I hold you for ransom?"

"My father the king," said Bird-Dropping, "will not pay. He will attack."

"Yes," confirmed Sunday. "He will come with his men and kill you all. He'll tan your hides to use as shoe leather, feed your flesh to his tigers, and carve up your bones for toothpicks."

Several of the thieves looked at each other uncomfortably.

"If you are lying," said the chief, "I cannot allow you to leave knowing that this cave is our hideout. But if you are telling the truth, I cannot afford to have you found here." He motioned to several of his men. "Take them and throw them in the pit. Let the dog take care of them."

The men carried Bird-Dropping and Sunday farther back into the cave. Deep growling and snarling sounded from a hole in the floor, and the stench of a filthy dog filled the air. The men lit a ring of torches around the hole, and then with no further ado, they threw Bird-Dropping and Sunday down into the pit.

How deep was the pit? Was there a big dog down there? Did the pit have another way out? These are all good questions, my child, and if you have patience they will all be answered.

Bird-Dropping and Sunday fell ten feet to the bottom of the pit. Because the floor was covered in grime and muck, Bird-Dropping stopped falling just short of hitting the ground. Sunday was not so lucky, and winced in pain from the force of the fall.

The two of them got to their feet and looked around.

Two large eyes glowed red in the flickering torchlight. The eyes came closer, and the light revealed a large dog. A very large dog. The largest dog there ever was before or has been since. It opened its mouth wide enough to swallow

Bird-Dropping whole, revealing huge yellowed teeth. The dog growled and came toward Bird-Dropping and Sunday. From around the edge of the pit, the thieves cheered the dog on.

Clutching each other's hands, Bird-Dropping and Sunday backed away until they found themselves trapped between the dirt wall of the pit and the snarling, slobbering hound.

Then the dog stopped, sniffing the air in puzzlement. It could see two people, but Bird-Dropping was so clean he had no scent at all. For a dog, such a thing is a great mystery. It finally decided to ignore the scentless thing and went to bite Sunday.

Seeing his sister in danger, Bird-Dropping did the only thing he could to prevent the dog from biting her: he leapt into the dog's mouth.

The dog was surprised by this. Usually its meals tried to avoid being eaten, but the scentless boy was halfway inside its mouth. The dog was not going to argue with that, so it closed its jaws to bite the boy in half.

Except its jaws would not close all the way. It bit down harder, and one of its teeth broke off. Try as it might, the dog could not bite into Bird-Dropping, because its teeth were filthy.

After several minutes, the dog finally gave up trying to bite. Instead, while the thieves whistled and stomped their approval, the dog raised its head up, opened its jaws wide, and swallowed Bird-Dropping whole.

Poor Sunday was left alone with the dog, and she began to cry. She cried more for the loss of her brother than she did for her own fear. Fortunately, the dog, having eaten its fill for now, ignored Sunday and lay down to take a nap.

Sunday sat down and tried to think what to do next.

But the dog could not sleep, for inside its stomach there was an uncomfortable wriggling.

Bird-Dropping told himself not to be scared, but it was the first time in his life he'd been in complete darkness. Travelling in the shoe of the giant who carried the Sun meant Bird-Dropping had never seen night time. After a moment's thought, Bird-Dropping decided to try crawling back up the dog's gullet to see if he could get out when the dog opened its mouth again.

He crawled and crawled. He didn't think he had come this far down the creature's throat, but he kept crawling.

And suddenly he found himself emerging from the dog's rear end, near a large pile of dog-doo.

"Bird-Dropping! You're alive!" declared Sunday.

"I must have gotten turned around in the darkness," said Bird-Dropping as he jumped to the ground, still clean as can be despite the path he had taken.

The dog just whimpered, making no move to attack them. Having someone crawl through your gut is not pleasant, or so it is said by those who know.

Sunday glanced up at the entrance to the pit, which was too high above for them to reach — even if it weren't surrounded by jeering thieves. "How will we get out?" she asked. "That's the only exit."

Bird-Dropping walked to the wall of the pit and reached out to touch it.

The dirt parted before his clean fingers, of course, because if dirt isn't dirty, what is?

"Take my hand and follow me," said Bird-Dropping.

And as they walked forward, the ground opened up before them until they safely emerged from the earth. But they could tell from the position of the Sun that Merklas had already stepped away. The shoe that had been their home was gone, along with their family.

Bird-Dropping and Sunday began walking to the nearest town.

"After all that has happened, I will give you a new name," said Sunday.

Bird-Dropping was happy, as he did not like his name. "Not Dog-Doo, please."

"No," said Sunday. "I will not name you Dog-Doo."

"And not something like Clean-Boy just because I am clean," said Bird-Dropping.

"No," said Sunday. "Your cleanliness may have given you the power to save me, but it was the strength of your heart that gave you the will. I will call you Strongheart."

And he was known as Strongheart from that day forth. And by that name he grew up to become a great hero. A very great hero. The greatest hero there ever was before or has been since.

Did Strongheart and Sunday ever see their family again? Did Strongheart ever find his real parents? How did he defeat the wily Gruntlebeast and milk its sea of teats in order to become king of all Voralia? These are all good questions, my child, and if you have patience they will all be answered.

But not today.

MANGO DICTIONARY AND THE DRAGON QUEEN OF CONTRACT EVOLUTION

Gareth Owens

"Dragons." The Waylarn paused for effect. "Lots of them ... all over the place."

The Lady Mango formed one eyebrow into a perfect arch as she listened.

"Interesting," she said. "And what exactly is it that you expect me to do about it?"

The Waylarn winced, visibly nerving himself up to his diplomatic task.

"When you were banished from Earth, it was always said that you were fiddling with sorcery."

"The word, Waylarn, is meddling, not fiddling." She fixed him with a gaze of razor sharp green steel. "Mango Dictionary does not *fiddle* with anything." The courtier winced again.

"I'm sorry, milady. I will keep that in mind."

"You would best be advised to do exactly that, Waylarn. The *Cantus Belli* may be an old ship, but she is an old *Earth* ship, and directly above this pathetic pig-farm you call a colony. Are you familiar with the saying, 'Newbility needs no reason'?"

"Yes, milady." The Waylarn lowered his gaze. "But Contract Evolution has become your own personal fiefdom. We pay you our tribute. We are your people, your thanes, can we not come to you with our grievances in time of need?"

The Lady Mango Stargazy in Illness Conceived under the Purple Skies of Magdalene Dictionary (the third) slowly realized that the pudgy, badly-dressed and sweaty individual in the coms field was doing what no other man in her entire life had ever done. He was standing up to her.

She lay back on her chez-tongue, momentarily admiring the courage of the man. He knew that the *Cantus Belli* was linked to her every whim. He must have been completely aware that the vast imperial relic that hung over his world had the power to swat him as if he was nothing but an insect, and yet, he still had the bravery to press his case.

"Very well, Waylarn, your pleas have moved me and I will investigate."

"Oh milady, th…"

His thanks ended abruptly as a large-bore blast-cannon tracked the com signal back to its point of origin and wiped the odious little commoner from the face of existence. The Lady Mango even allowed herself a wry and somewhat self-satisfied smile at the thought of all his brave little atoms now being wafted around the skies of the disgusting, and apparently dragon ridden, world of Contract Evolution.

However, she would investigate. Her word was as good as a sworn vow. The vast gothic gold hull of the *Cantus Belli* stretched like a waking cat. Statues sighed and corridors constricted. Energy fields fluxed and flexed as the old ship, called the Hammer of Freedom by the long defeated Republican Star Force of French Mars, felt the desires within the Lady Mango and reconfigured herself to be more suited to the Lady's whim.

Malleable metal morphed - mutating, melting and melding. Mango moved, the long train of her dress rustling as it flowed liquid and seamlessly into the organic marble deck. Sumptuous, gold and black, the extruded material that flowed from the old ship swirled around the Lady like the surging coastal sea-foam thrown against the ebony rocks of her birthworld. The *Cantus Belli* clothed her with itself, and in return the Lady Mango became the heart of the island in the sky.

They had been joined at the soul since Mango had reached puberty. The *Cantus Belli* had accepted her as its own flesh, and the Lady Mango had become the soul of the leviathan. The conjoining of the two had been destined since the genetic compatibility of her parents had been calculated from across all the great houses of the Empire, and the Emperor himself had consented to be her cousin.

That had all been before the fall.

Mango began to descend, a bubble of decking forming around her as the *Cantus Belli* lowered her gently through the structure of the ship. She was transported like a morsel trapped in the vacuole of an amoeba, until with a sigh, the *Cantus Belli* lovingly opened up the rooms of the shuttle collection.

Drifting between pillars of gold, torches burning in recesses, Mango laid herself on a viewing throne and the *Cantus Belli* wafted shuttles before her until she spotted one that suited her mood.

A sphere of flowing information crystallised, becoming solid around her, and she became entwined with its fabric. Mango Dictionary and the *Cantus Belli* became almost distinct and separate. The shuttle was kissed into space, a bubble that contained all that mattered in the universe to the relic of times long forgotten.

The Lady Mango stood as if on a magic carpet, in her left hand a single crystal ball, the perfect sphere of Contract Evolution filling her vision as she left the imperial leviathan behind.

The planet before her was mud brown from pole to pole, and the reason for the mud brown colour was that Contract Evolution was a sea of mud from pole to pole. The *Cantus Belli* could not completely explain the roundness of Contract Evolution but the Lady Mango had been satisfied with a 'best guess', which was that at some point in the fledgling planet's history a near miss with another object had melted the entire surface, and Contract Evolution had become the roundest and nearest to spherical planet ever discovered by the spreading rash that was humanity.

Contract Evolution had no basins and no depths but it did have a lot of water, which covered the entire surface of the world to a depth of a few inches. As Mango floated downwards, descending like a vampire on a virgin neck, she was again struck by the perfect complexion of this world. It swirled like an opal with shades of brown, the perfect white clouds marbling the marble; a world that looked like a cake, or a perfect smooth gem.

Mango scanned the world with her gaze, looking for anything that might resemble a permanent way-mark. But there was nothing. The colonies were simple rafted affairs drifting over the placid mud-sea of Contract Evolution, straining the planet-covering soup for whatever could be sold on the interstellar auction sites.

The Lady Mango penetrated the atmosphere, her crystal sphere of a magic carpet now a projectile that seared the sky as a bullet of pure flame. The expression on her face was as serene as her heart, which saw the approaching world with nothing but a slight sharpening of appetite.

The shuttle was filled with the music of angels chanting over the pits of hell and the demons below responding. Chiming and dramatic, she fell on Contract Evolution, looking for a dragon, or some dragons, or even lots of dragons. But what she really wanted to find was an explanation.

The Waylarn's image had originated near the North Swirl, the part of the planet where the mud of the surface swirled like the locks of Mango's perfect crown.

She stared into the crystal ball that she held and mapped the planet below. The eyes of the old ship above her roved the surface looking for the tell-tale signs of living beings, and the *Cantus Belli* found them, in their thousands scattered all across the world. Yet not one was anything other than those species that humanity had carried between the stars.

Had the Waylarn sacrificed his life for a joke? The Lady Mango's perfect eyes changed to a deep violet, cat's iris's to match her tiger mood. If this was some attempt to fool her, then she had the claws to make sure that no such cancer could take root within her fiefdom.

The crystal surface of the shuttle faded as to be invisible and Mango flew above the planet-wide sea. She stood regal but ready to strike. Her desire before it reached thought was enough to steer her course. This was what her life had always been like; before she knew that she wanted something, it had already been provided. That had been what had led to her downfall and why she and the *Cantus Belli* now skulked in the outer fringes of the poorer sections of the empire.

Her fury surged around inside her, a roiling ocean of brimstone that would not let her rest. The resentment of her cousin and those courtiers that had consigned her to the outer darkness burned in her heart, a magma core of revenge looking for a weak spot to erupt and blast away at all that had confined her.

Her eyes scanned the surface of the world. "Dragons, lots of them, all over the place". That was what he had said, and she had made the trip to find them, and there were no dragons, and she had already dealt with the Waylarn. Well, she would have to find someone else to punish for this deception, she thought.

The surface of the mud below began to stir. Ripples and rivulets gave the uniform brown the appearance of having been combed. Then a hump began to form down the centre of the disturbance. Mango was now a mere twenty metres from the world, and the disturbed area stretched as far as her unaided eye could see.

The brown mud now had a current. Mango followed the flow. A gradient was beginning to form and the current became a torrent, brown water cascading down a sudden hill. Then, from the mud, Mango could see the ripples of muscle, spines erupting in a kilometre long row ahead of her. She climbed into the sky to get a better look at what was happening around her.

She was unused to fear, unknown to it and it to her. The *Cantus Belli*, her immortal and all powerful lover and ally, was there as a shield; an impenetrable armour through which not even the awareness of a danger could pass. So it was that when she realized she was witnessing the birth of a dragon of geological scale, ripping itself from the very fabric of the world below, she was charting unknown emotional territory.

Bowel loosening in size, the great drake spread her wings. Mango could see flight muscles dragging the membranous sails free of the mud-ocean.

The Lady Mango now stood braced against the back wall of her shuttle sphere, her arms spread out wide, and she wondered what the sound that she could hear was before realising it was her own panting. Colour flashed across the leathery skin of the dragon, gleaming iridescent scales taking on the patterns of butterflies' wings. She shimmered like oily water and rainbow skies, and tens of kilometres away the neck began to rise up, long and slender and strong, roped and laced with sinew and more powerful than the attraction of distant atoms.

Set atop the pillar of dragon flesh, Mango realized that she was looking at the back of the freshly born dragon's head. Great scaled horns rose above the brow and pointed ears pricked with obvious alert and vicious intelligence.

Mango stood on her magic carpet feeling completely exposed to the might of this sudden change in the universe. Microscopic, an insect to be flicked in to oblivion without consideration or consequence.

Then, as if hearing a sound behind her, the great dragon twisted her head on that gigantic tower of a neck and Mango found herself under the scrutiny of a vast wheel of a bejewelled eye.

Above her the *Cantus Belli* could feel the depth and urgency of her fear, yet those ancient eyes, built at the beginning of human civilisation and never bettered, could see nothing. Mango screamed, and the *Cantus Belli* shuddered at the sound. Weapons formed on the planetward surface of the ancient vessel, erupting bolts of energy and fury. The sky around the Lady Mango burned with a hard rain of the Earth's imperial rage. Cannonade and twisting pillars of energy criss-crossed the back of the dragon behemoth. The lady looked into the dragon's eyes and saw that the vast beast was laughing at her. Laughing at Mango Dictionary.

The dragon turned. Contract Evolution shook and quaked under the strain of supporting the queen of all dragons. She clawed the globe, and with a supersonic flick of wings and tail, she faced the Lady Mango. The dragon queen rose up on her haunches, wrapping her tail around herself as if it were a snake and spreading her wings so as to block out the sky. And then the dragon took a breath.

Mango knew about dragons, humans carried dragons with them in their genes. It had always been as if somehow humans were aware of the Great Drakes through some thin curtain of reality. As if they were always next door, separated from us by nothing more substantial than flimsy gauze. Mango knew that the dragon summoned gale that filled the lungs of the beast would erupt again in a tsunami of flame, a tempest of fire, the fury of the dragon made fierily manifest. She also knew, without even a hint of doubt, that the shuttle and all the might of the *Cantus Belli* would not, could not protect her from the rage of this ruthless draconian queen.

With a smile of malicious intent, the dragon began to swoop down on the Lady Mango. Mango heard herself scream, the music still playing in her shuttle, and her scream, ripped from a part of her soul she had never known, was a perfect high note and fitted to her symphony of terror as if written to it.

Black smoke escaped the fumaroles of the dragon's nostrils, forced aside by the dragon swoop as the Queen came for the Lady.

Finally the Lady Mango crystallised her desire to be elsewhere and the shuttle began to climb into the heavens. She ran away. Never before, not even in her dreams, had she had need to flee, but now she knew the desire to run. She felt its power and she gave into it. The shuttle shot into the deep-dark of the sky like a tear of crystallized, burning, whimpering dread. Behind her the dragon leapt into the heavens. Great leathery sails of wings, each one the size of a continent, flapped twice, releasing tornadoes across the brown sea. The tornadoes became waterspouts, vertical twisting walls of water, towering above the flimsy rafts of the colonists.

Mango looked over her shoulder, her open mouthed and breathless terror coalescing as a fist of unshakable pain in her chest. The jaws of the dragon mother stretched wide, each tooth the size of a mountain.

Then, with a feeling as if the whole universe was laughing at her, Mango's eyes saw but could not comprehend that the dragon queen was disintegrating into a flock of thousands of cackling dragonoras, then each dragonora split into hundreds of dragons of all colours and temperatures. The dragons split into iridescent dragonettes, and then the dragonettes into a rainbow of draglet drops, and finally the cloud of draglets faded from view like a subsiding chuckle.

Mango looked towards the dark. The *Cantus Belli* filled the whole of the sky above as it rushed to gather her up. With the urgency of a mother sweeping up a fleeing child, the shuttle was absorbed into the fabric of the great ship. Mango, shaken and shocked, slumped - sliding slowly she subsided, still sobbing, struggling to understand the scale of what she had seen. The wreck of the Lady was carried through the halls of the ship to her throne room. The *Cantus Belli* held her safe, and without knowing that she had wanted it, the old Earth ship kicked away from the gravity well of Contract Evolution and headed into the deep-dark.

Far below, on the surface of the Contract Evolution and half a world away from the site of his apparent demise, the Waylarn smiled as he disconnected from the device. It was ancient, and no one could say whether it was alien or human made, but it could summon up a fair old dragon when it wanted to.

LODE STARS

Lavie Tidhar

The Illuminati starship *Trinity* was three light years away from the Orbitals and decelerating when the message reached Mikhaila Petrova that her father had died. For her it was only a month since she had last seen him, but that time was relative: back home in the Orbitals, over three years had passed.

He must have died almost as soon as she left for the Third Eye. She stared at the screen and re-ran the message, watching her aunt as she spoke. There was a new, discreet scar under her aunt's left eye and her skin bulged, just slightly, below the ear. Adapted Martian bioware. She must have got *that* pretty quickly too.

'Mikhaila,' Aunt Alexandra said, 'your father's gone into God's eye.' She stared into the camera and nodded slowly. Her lips were surprisingly fat in the thin, ascetic face. 'I know this will come as a shock.'

Three light-years away, Mikhaila stared at her aunt's image and the same sense of dislike filled her that always did where her father's older sister was concerned. Dislike, followed swiftly by an anger that tried to mask the pain beneath.

On screen, Alexandra shrugged, looking momentarily helpless. 'He was alone in the Cyclop around the eye, meditating. In recent years, Mikki, your father had developed some strange ideas. I must confess I was relieved when you took command of the *Trinity* and took her to Third Eye. Your father's ideas … were a cause for concern. When you left he began to spend much of his time in the Cyclop, skirting close to the gravitational pull of the Eye. He must have simply come too close, found out too late that he couldn't turn back.' She sighed and said, 'I know he went gladly when he realized, knowing he will be seen by God.'

Mikhaila sat alone and watched Aunt Alexandra twist on screen. That sudden piousness at the end was unlike the woman she remembered, and Mikhaila wondered numbly what else had changed back home in the last three years.

'Your father's gone into God's eye' – the polite Illuminati way of saying 'he's dead.' But her father really had gone into God's eye. She bit her lower lip until she felt pain, tasting a drop of blood like the taste of dull metal. Father, alone in the tiny Cyclop, suddenly too close to the gravitational field; the brief realization that there is no going back. Then the tides, tearing him and the ship into individual atoms, sucking them in until they passed the event horizon and disappeared forever from the visible universe. She didn't think it would hurt, much, being torn apart like this. But then again she couldn't know. When an Illuminati was sent to the Eye it was a funereal occasion, and the tides tore only at already-dead flesh, while the mourners watched from the Orbitals and performed the rituals and, later, got drunk.

'Don't come back,' Aunt Alexandra said on screen. 'There is nothing that you can do. Mikki...' Did the voice quaver a little? 'I'm sorry.'

The recording ceased and the screen faded back into being a wall. Mikhaila sat back and thought of her father again, alone as he was swallowed by the black hole. But for her father to die this way just didn't make sense. There was no way the Cyclop would be unable to determine the safety parameters around the Eye. So what had really happened? Why had her father died?

Her throat felt sore, tingled with swallowed tears. She stared at the wall for a long moment more before rising, and stepped into the corridor outside, heading to the ship's control room.

*

The *Trinity*'s deceleration brought it down from ninety-nine point ninety-nine percent of the speed of light to a more conventional ten percent. At this speed, time dilation still affected the crew but the differences between ship time and that of Third Eye's Orbitals were minimal. Mikhaila felt the pressure that had built up over the past month amongst the crew begin to dissipate when the screen lit up with an image of the Orbitals that wasn't Doppler-shifted. Three years, in the space of a month. It was a difficult transition to make.

The Orbitals ringed the Third Eye like dark clams, a wide chain of habitats worn around the neck of the black hole. Lights burned from a thousand human dwellings and local net traffic was rambunctious. And yet the chain was incomplete, and many of the Orbitals appeared to be drifting away – like a miniature Diaspora, Mikhaila thought. On screen the view changed, zoomed away from the Eye onto the star field beyond, and was then replaced by the eye-and-pyramid symbol.

'Incoming message,' Rochiro Yuki announced from her communications Conch. 'From Grandmistress Ortega of Third Eye.' She paused, then added, 'Time delay is currently at eight point five minutes.'

'Put her on,' Mikhaila said, and a moment later Grandmistress Ortega's blunt, nut-brown face appeared on the wide screen. The Grandmistress wore an organic eye-patch that seemed to crawl over her face and it startled Mikhaila, having just seen another Grandmistress who also carried evidence of new Martian bioware augmentation. She filed it away in her mind. Nothing the Grand Lodge members did was likely to be a coincidence.

Ortega didn't waste time on small talk: she introduced herself briskly before launching into the real reason for the call. 'Captain Petrova,' she said, 'you arrive at an inauspicious time. The Eye has been causing us some considerable concern in the past year, with increased emissions of Hawking radiation and an increase in gravitational force that have forced us to a distance from the Eye we have not had to take for a millennium. I understand –' her right, unaugmented eye stared directly into the camera so that she appeared to be looking down directly at Mikhaila – 'that you are here to conduct several specialised experiments in the vicinity of the Eye. When you left, there was no need to inquire more closely as to the nature of the experiments.' The eye blinked. The Martian eye-patch rippled like jelly over the left. 'That is no longer the case. I expect a full operations plan to be broadcast to me immediately. You will now direct your ship to the Grand Lodge Orbital where you will be my guests until a decision has been made whether to allow you access to the Eye.' She stopped, blinked. Mikhaila watched as right eye closed and left eye rippled. It made her want to punch the Martian eye-patch, the way one squashes a leech. 'I may have a different assignment for you.'

She disappeared, replaced on screen by the eye-and-pyramid logo.

'What the hell did that mean?' Sandor seethed from his Conch. His head stuck out of the immersion tank and he peered at Mikhaila with the slight bafflement that seemed to always surround the tall scientist.

'I expect some of the people living around Third Eye are becoming concerned enough to think of a little trip,' Mikhaila said. She had to force herself to concentrate: a mental image of her father being torn apart with the Cyclop kept enveloping her mind. 'To Homelight, most likely.'

'She can't *commandeer* the ship,' Sandor protested. 'Just so people can run away to a *world!*'

Like all Orbital dwellers he held those of Homelight, the Illuminati's only planetoid, with a mixture of hidden envy and openly-displayed contempt. Mikhaila remembered her one visit to Homelight for her initiation ceremony; all that she remembered clearly was the one view of the impossibly-tall, lizard-green pyramids that rose like volcanoes from the surface of the world. Homelight had no atmosphere; it was nothing more than a wandering moon until it was found by the Illuminati and dragged back to the three Eyes, and Mikhaila spent her entire time there in a small part of the Grand Lodge Pyramid, only granted that one fleeting look at the world from above. '*Grandmistress* Ortega can do what she wants,' Mikhaila said, a little stiffly. 'If she decides to send us off to Homelight or Second Eye or even back home, there's absolutely nothing we can do about it.'

'Well *I* can't see it coming to that,' Rochiro said. 'Though it isn't such a bad idea, you know. We could charter the ship and get ourselves a round trip to the world.' The sound of laughter emerged from her Conch. 'Everybody knows

Third Eyers are rich.'

'We'll see,' Mikhaila said. Then she told them about her father.

*

The Grand Lodge Orbital was a small moon with its own ring of smaller orbiting habitats. Mikhaila was surprised it was so close to the Eye. She was also concerned.

The *Trinity* decelerated gently into the Third Eye system until reaching a near-stationary position on the edge of the Grand Lodge's hangers-on: some of them had evidently been around for a very long time. A nearby orbital was a miniature stellar system composed of three hollowed-out asteroids, a Ring and two more modern – though still several centuries old – constructed orbitals, all linked together into a makeshift web. There was even a small pyramid, growing on the back of the smallest asteroid like a bright green tumour.

If Ortega was telling the truth about the recent, unexplained activity of the Eye, then why were the Grand Lodge and its followers so close to the Eye's gravitational pull? And if Ortega, for whatever reason, wasn't telling the truth, and there *was* no danger, then the question changed and became a big *why*. Why would Ortega lie about the activity of the Eye? No, Mikhaila decided, Grandmistress Ortega would not lie about that and, in fact, Sandor had already confirmed the unusual activity of the Eye as they decelerated, as did Rochiro's analysis of the local net traffic. But perhaps she wasn't telling them all of the truth, and she knew more than she was admitting or telling. Mikhaila wondered if the Grandmistress knew what the small crew of the *Trinity* really wanted to achieve here, three long light years away from home. It was a game she wasn't sure how well she could play. For now, she filed away the speculations and concentrated on the ride to the orbital.

She and Sandor got into their individual Cyclops; she always thought of the release from the ship as the image of a fish, blowing bubbles. She and Sandor were the bubbles: Rochiro had renounced flesh life several years before and had become a Conch, living entirely inside the immersion tank and she rarely now left the ship.

'I'll pick up some information about stuff back home,' she said. 'As well as the local situation. You keep your ears open too.'

A hole opened in the Grand Lodge orbital, and the two Cyclops were swallowed by it and entered one of the orbital's giant hangars. A delegation of two recent Initiates welcomed them and led the way to the meeting with Ortega.

In person, the Grandmistress was surprisingly short, and her Martian bioware augmentation even more repulsive. Mikhaila's father had never trusted the biological artefacts created from the forced evolution of the few microbiological traces discovered on Mars, back in pre-Exodus days. The alien genetic code itself was fascinating – Mikhaila had taken a few basic modules of Martian Bio Programming her first year at the Magdalen Orbiter – but the results always carried with them a strange, alien sense that made her feel uncomfortable.

'Captain Petrova,' Ortega said. Her hand was brown and calloused and her grip was firm as she shook Mikhaila's hand. The eye-patch rippled as she spoke. 'I am sorry to hear about your loss.'

Surprise mingled with shock; perhaps seeing that in Mikhaila's face, the Grandmistress added, 'I expect I received the message from First Eye at the same time as you. Again, I am sorry. Your aunt Alexandra was very fond of your father.'

Mikhaila forced herself to smile, said something about 'dear aunt Alexandra,' while in her mind she saw again the unwelcome image of her father, sucked into the Eye. 'I was not aware you knew each other.'

'No?' Something in Ortega's voice suggested she did not quite believe Mikhaila. 'We were initiated into the Mysteries together on Homelight. Your aunt is now a powerful figure at the First Eye Grand Lodge; you must know we keep a permanent feed between the Eyes.'

'Of course,' Mikhaila said. 'I'm sorry. The news…it is something of a shock.'

Grandmistress Ortega nodded. 'I understand.' A small smile touched the corners of her mouth and she touched Mikhaila lightly on her shoulder. 'If you need to talk please come to me. The loss of your father is a loss to all Illuminati.'

Mikhaila nodded, biting down on a reply. Instead, she asked, 'Have you had a chance to look at the research proposal I forwarded?'

Ortega's thin smile withdrew. 'Yes. I'm afraid that under the current circumstances it would not be advisable.'

Anger warmed Mikhaila's face. 'And why not?'

An unreadable expression settled on Ortega's face. 'Because right now I don't need any more casualties like your father.'

The words hung between them, riding a tense, growing silence as the two women locked eyes. 'I demand access to the Eye,' Mikhaila said. Her voice was soft, barely audible, but it affected the Grandmistress like a physical blow.

'You can demand nothing,' Ortega retorted. 'Don't forget your position, captain. Do you reject the authority of the Lodge?'

'I spent three *years* travelling here,' Mikhaila said. 'I will *not* turn back now.'

The thin smile returned to Ortega's lined face. 'I'm afraid,' she said, equally softly, 'that you don't really have a choice at all.' She turned away from Mikhaila and gestured to a wide screen where the Orbitals were displayed from a distant camera. 'The Eye is growing,' she revealed quietly. 'Only by tiny increments, but it is growing as if it is being fed matter on a large scale. *Something* is causing that, and as we don't know what then the Grand Lodge has no choice but to see it as a potentially hostile activity.'

'Hostile?' Disgust almost made her choke. 'What could possibly threaten the Illuminati?'

On Ortega's face the Martian eye-patch shivered and began to migrate across her skin, revealing a grotesque hole where her left eye should have been. 'I don't know,' she said. She had pitched her voice low still, but the anger in it was unmistakable. 'And until I do, no one – and that means *no one*, captain - is allowed access to the Eye. Do I make myself understood?'

The eye-patch now nestled in the space between Ortega's left shoulder and her neck. It looked like a sleepy, obese beetle.

'Yes,' Mikhaila said. Cold settled in the bottom of her stomach and spread, enveloping her until she felt as if she were made entirely of ice. 'Quite, quite clear.'

*

'Is the woman mad?' Rochiro said loudly in Mikhaila's ear. Mikhaila was in her allocated rooms at the Grand Lodge: she didn't plan to stay there long. 'She is going directly against the Mysteries!'

'I don't think she is mad,' Mikhaila sub-vocalized. 'But I do wonder what she's playing at. I noticed all the local feeds aimed at the Eye don't appear to be operating. What's net traffic like?'

'The same,' Rochiro admitted. 'Everything is being re-routed on direct links cutting out the Godfeeds - narrow beam, minimal loss. It's strange. Much more efficient, obviously, but how will God see us?'

'I don't think it's God that's being blinded,' Mikhaila said. She massaged her face, feeling a growing pain in the bridge of her nose. 'I think...I think my father was successful.' She didn't complete her thought aloud, conscious that the conversation was most likely monitored. *I think the Eye is talking back.*

'How's Sandor?' Rochiro said, changing the subject.

Mikhaila laughed. 'Grumpy. He demanded permission to run his experiments from Grandmistress Ortega. *Demanded.* It didn't go very well from there.'

'What *are* we going to do, captain?'

'I have an idea,' Mikhaila said. The pain spread up to her eyes now. 'But we'll talk about it back on the ship. Meantime, how are the backpackers?'

'Most of them are gone already,' Rochiro replied. 'I mentioned a possible Homelight flight and a few are sticking around for it. Willing to pay too.'

'Is that Ran one of them?'

'Raz. Yeah.'

Mikhaila wondered briefly about Rochiro's complicated sex life, then shook the thought from her head. Who – or *how* – her comms officer spent her off time with was none of her business. And it was always good to have a few backpackers around, if only for morale.

'Ortega didn't mention anything to me. Yet,' Mikhaila said. 'I have a meeting with her in a few hours. I'm going to try and get some sleep first. Hopefully she'll let us go after that.'

'Sleep well then,' Rochiro said, and the connection ended.

Mikhaila lay back on the bed and thought about her father; and about what it was that she thought he had done.

*

She felt only a little better after her sleep, and worse after her meeting with Ortega. But now, as she was gliding through space in her Cyclop – a round, compact craft whose shell could be made to allow through harmless light, thus turning the entire vehicle transparent – and saw the *Trinity* she felt better. Smaller craft hovered all over the *Trinity*'s shell, attaching themselves like flies to flesh. Ships came and went in a complicated dance: there were never that many starships and whenever one went cross-system (or cross-Eyed, which as a joke dated back nearly two millennia) it had plenty to carry. The two Cyclops wove themselves into the elaborate dance and soon Mikhaila and Sandor were standing back in the command room of the *Trinity* with Rochiro.

'Ortega wants us to go to Homelight,' Sandor said the moment he saw her. He blinked at the command room as if searching for a place to vent anger. 'I'd say it was just her way of getting rid of us, but there were a hell of a lot of people came up to me asking about a place.'

'Three,' Mikhaila said, and Sandor grimaced. 'It's indicative of a wider trend,' he argued.

Mikhaila smiled.

'So what's the plan, captain?' Rochiro wondered. 'Seeing as we can't dump anything into the Eye for the foreseeable future...'

'No,' Mikhaila said. 'We can't. But we *can* monitor the Hawking radiation that's being emitted.'

'You think...?' Rochiro said, and Mikhaila asked, 'Can you do it?'

'Sure. Don't know if it would be political to send out a few probes but I can probably get all the data directly off of Third Eye Mirror.'

'Just make sure you confirm its authenticity,' Sandor warned darkly. 'Something doesn't feel right about any of this.'

'Yes, *sir*,' Rochiro said. 'Captain, is there anything else?'

'Yes,' Mikhaila said. 'I want you to delay the *Trinity* for as long as you can. Come up with some technical problems to keep us stationary. And find me someone on the, um, *unofficial* channels who knows about Martian biotech.'

'Might take a few days to make a contact,' Rochiro said. Mikhaila thought about the Grandmistress' eye-patch, of her aunt's own new augmentation hidden beneath her skin. 'That's fine,' she replied. 'Just make sure it's not traceable.'

'I'll see what I can do.' The silence that followed from the communications Conch carried a strong sense of irritation. Mikhaila almost smiled: Rochiro was convinced that as a Conch she was a true Illuminati, one of the few truly Enlightened who always knew what was *really* going on. She'd be eating up bandwidth following anything she could sniff out. 'I'm sorry,' she said, feeling suddenly tired again, 'you know what you're doing.'

The three of them fell into a silence. It was the comfortable silence of people who knew each other well, and Mikhaila felt that she was setting something raw and unpredictable into that unit, *her* unit, when she broke it and said, 'Sandor, I want you to wake up Leibniz.'

*

The Martian expert lived in Ghostown.

It took seven ship-days (by now aligned with Third Eye's own calendar-time arrangement) to locate him. When Rochiro at last told Mikhaila, she had sounded sheepish.

'A *hobbyist*?' Mikhaila had exclaimed. 'I said unofficial channels and you got me some guy who plays with a backyard evolution kit?'

'Mr Alvarez,' Roshiro had said, each word enunciated clearly, 'is an *expert* on Martian bio-coding. An expert, moreover, who is not affiliated with any official Lodge corporations.'

Mikhaila nodded. Under the circumstances she couldn't really complain. 'Fine. When can I see him?'

The hidden Rochiro, the part of her that was flesh and blood, might have smiled. 'Any time you like.' Then she told her where Mr. Alvarez lived.

Cocooned in the Cyclop, Mikhaila now watched as the distant lights of Ghostown lit up a complex – yet essentially random – pattern against the darkness of Eyeless space. They twinkled in and out of existence, inscribing messages for God that had no meaning to anyone but, perhaps, the ghosts.

The Cyclop floated closer and Ghostown came into naked-eye view; Mikhaila drew in breath as the giant, elongated structure filled up her field of vision. It was like a rock the size of a moon that had been stretched across space into a wide baguette shape, pan-fried and old - even from a distance she could see that the outer shell was crawling with insects. A black-metal beetle emitting ionised particles from its rear approached the Cyclop and for a moment the view blanked. The beetle was the size of her fist. In that brief glimpse it looked fat and well-fed.

When the screen cleared, a hole was opening in the side of the rock, expelling out both air and mechanoid insects; she heard their angry buzzing as they flooded the local channels. The Cyclop slid into the opening.

Ghostown's rotation created only a very low gravity. Mikhaila found herself inside a tomb-like space, almost floating in the thin air. It smelled dry, with only a distant taste of something human, like smoke or the lingering traces of frying onion. Here there were no bugs: all around her and as far away as she could see stood a vast and open forest of columns that rose from the rocky ground, gleaming in hues of matt black and cold metallic blue, and disappeared into the impossibly-high ceiling.

She took another breath; the ghosts began whispering to her.

Their whispers had an almost physical touch, and as she walked away from the Cyclop they grew it tone and volume until some of the trapped souls screeched and others begged her: to touch the columns, to let them ride her body, to help them. Some of the columns shifted and changed their look, revealing a hidden, virtual world beneath, and some of the ghosts manifested on the makeshift screens, some men and some women, and some no longer recognisable as human.

She had never before seen a ghost, and she found the experience distressing. Ghostown was the end result of an ancient belief: back in the pre-Exodus solar system of which Earth was a part, many people – some of them Illuminati – talked about the possibility of an event they called a Singularity, and of something else called Upload culture. The idea was that human minds could be transported to digital systems: neuron-networks copied, neuron by painstaking neuron, until an exact, digital copy of the mind resided in a virtual environment where it could live like a god, at least a demi-god.

The idea was not impossible, and so, some centuries after the Illuminati fleet discovered the three Eyes and settled around three *real* singularities, a splinter group around Third Eye built the complex that eventually became known as Ghostown. It was an honourable experiment: the men and women who worked on it had wanted to transcend as a way of coming closer to God, that unexplained, unknown force that resided in the ur-universe from which all other universes grew, and watched this particular universe – so the Illuminati reasoned – through the only eyes it had: the singularities that hid at the heart of every black hole.

'Mikhaila Petrova?'

The voice startled her. It was deep and strangely homely, and the man who stepped out of what appeared to her for a moment as just another screen was small and deeply tanned, with sparse white hair and deep, brown eyes. 'Mr. Alvarez?'

He nodded. 'Shmuel,' he said. He gestured. 'What do you think of it?'

'It's...' Mikhaila began, and then wasn't sure what answer he expected. 'Disconcerting.'

Shmuel Alvarez nodded. He stepped forward and, now that she could see him more clearly, Mikhaila discerned the patches of Martian bioware on his nearly-naked body. His body itself was muscled and seemed younger than his face, and he wore only a small loincloth that – she realized with a start – was not cloth but another Martian bio-construct. As she watched, the loincloth opened a lazy, inhuman eye and winked at her.

'It takes you that way,' Alvarez said quietly. 'Sometimes I think it would be merciful if we just pointed it at the Eye and sent the ghosts directly to God. But I am afraid that is not a course of action the Grand Lodge would ever tolerate. Come with me.'

He led Mikhaila through the cavern of columns, and all the time the ghosts whispered to her and cried for her to save them. She saw faces whose features were distinct and different from each other, who spoke in old dialects and laughed and cried and shouted her name, which they had picked up from Alvarez's speech.

She tried not to show how she felt. Disgust, which she hadn't expected to feel, and pity, which she had. The ghosts surprised her, and she couldn't tell why. They made her think of her father, and she wondered again about what she thought he tried to achieve, and if he, too, was a ghost in some form. The Illuminati who were involved in the Upload project did not consider that the human brain would have a problem existing in isolation, that it was evolved to function in a human body, and that sensory input – of a specific kind – was needed. In other words, a human brain needed a human body – and what happened when a mind was trapped in a virtual environment was apparent all around her.

'They killed themselves,' Alvarez said. 'The Upload process used a copy-and-erase approach, to make sure no one would be left behind. That ghost," he pointed at a column they were just passing; the fractured face of a once-beautiful woman stared at them from a thousand replicated shards, 'is now the only thing left of the woman she had once been.'

'Why live here, Mr. Alvarez?'

They had reached a clearing in the forest of columns. It was a wide space that was fenced by light, flexible walls that were stretched from column to column and formed ... a zoo. Mikhaila watched as strange compact bio-con-structs walked and hopped and crawled across the rocky floor; some climbed the columns while others formed groups that more often than not merged gradually into one blob of mass before splitting again into different shapes. A creature the size of a small child ambled towards her and from its mouth came the shriek of a ghost encased in new-found flesh.

'Because it's private, Captain Petrova,' Shmuel Alvarez explained, and his hands moved as if to encompass the entire mini-habitat he had created. 'And because I find there are inherent potentialities in the possible creation of a ghost-Martian interface.'

'Feel you ... touch you ... taste you ... smell you...' The possessed Martian construction moved towards Mikhaila and fell to all fours, developing an elongated snout in the process. 'Make love...' Its voice sounded suddenly forlorn and lost.

'Enough,' Alvarez commanded, and the ghost-ridden creature stiffened, then turned away without sound.

'You're not joking,' Mikhaila said. She looked at Alvarez's creation and held down a shudder. She'd prefer to deal with the Grandmistresses themselves.

'No,' Alvarez agreed. He led her to a small house erected in the centre of the clearing. When they got there she discovered the house was no more than a small room made of the same light material as the outer walls, and that it was empty. Alvarez closed the door. His loincloth shook and stretched itself around him, flesh-coloured and thin.

He tilted his head as if listening. Then, 'No,' he said again. 'A ghost-Martian interface is a possibility that has significant implications for the deeper Mysteries. Your father understood that well, Mikhaila.'

She drew back. 'How do you know my father?'

There was a mesh of fine wrinkles at the corners of Shmuel Alvarez's eyes and they made his smile seem sad. 'How do I know what he believed? Because I believe the same as him, Mikhaila. Because I, too, believe that there is life beyond the Eyes' event horizon.'

*

She woke up into darkness and the sweet faint smell of her lover's body pressed into her between the sheets. Ernesto's arm was lying on her chest, and when she pushed him off he muttered something intelligible and turned over.

Mikhaila rose and put on the loose informal trousers and shirt that was the sign of ship life; it made her smile, the thought of this super-advanced starship being piloted by people dressed in pyjamas.

The *Trinity* was on her way to Homelight, cargo hold converted to people-carrying. Beside the backpackers (Ernesto joined the ship at Third Eye while Rochiro's Raz remained with them, happy to follow Rochiro after his brief exploration of the Third Eye Orbitals) the ship thronged with Third Eye families who had decided to take the one and a half light years journey to the world. Mikhaila walked softly out of Ernesto's cabin and made her way through a service corridor (Crew Only) back to the control room, where Sandor waited.

'Leibniz's awake,' he said, and nodded to a corner of the room where the Other's avatar sat calmly in an old-fashioned armchair.

Starships did not, as a rule, need overwhelmingly powerful computers. The very first space probes sent from Earth seemed to manage, just about, with two 8-bit processors and the Illuminati designers appreciated that fact. Nevertheless, the *Trinity* did carry with it one piece of complex machinery: a quantum computer with a DNA-coded interface and its own fortified cadaver of hulk-metal. More than any human, Leibniz was conscious of the possibility of permanent death and was determined to have nothing to do with it.

Leibniz's avatar stood up as she came into the room. It was over six feet tall, a silver-skinned, bald mannequin whose sexless body was undraped by clothes. If humans feared being Uploaded, the Others feared the opposite: being trapped in a human body, being *Downloaded* seemed to them perverse and frightening, and would drive the being so confined into a dangerous process of fragmentation and insanity.

'Petrova,' Leibniz said. The voice came directly from the avatar's mouth, which did not move. Like most Others, Leibniz could communicate with people, running a sort of low-level expert system that mimicked a human personality, but as he had said to Petrova the one time, what was the point? Others did not evolve from biological bodies but in the vast and disembodied breeding grounds of digital code, and subsequently did not have the drives and emotions, flesh-bound, that formed a human character.

As usual, Leibniz went straight to the point. 'If there is a code hidden in the Hawking radiation then I can't find it.' The mannequin hesitated, and then said, 'Unless it is there and I can't see and understand it.'

Mikhaila thought about what Alvarez had told her, back on Ghostown. She expected Leibniz's next words.

'Petrova,' Leibniz said, and the voice coming from the mannequin changed, sounding like metal flashing in a dark room. 'Why is there a ghost on the ship?'
'Ah.'

The ghost was Alvarez's parting gift, as was the fat, amorphous Martian aug that she had left in Rochiro's capable, if proverbial, hands as soon as she could. She didn't imagine the Other had missed the fact, or its implications. But it was giving her the chance to argue: it was all that she could hope for.

'I do not wish to interface with biological matter.'

'It's only a different platform,' Mikhaila pointed out. She felt wide-awake; she had slept deep for the first time in months. 'It's *code*.'

'Running a crazed human ghost riding shotgun? Mikhaila, self-preservation alone would forbid me from trying.'

'Tell me.' Mikhaila stared at the avatar and it stared back, without expression. 'How long have you been an Illuminati?'

The voice lost its inflection, became flat. 'I came out of the breeding grounds about seven hundred years ago. I was initiated into the Mysteries shortly after.'

'Do you believe that singularities, as the only places where the laws of the universe do not apply, are windows into the ur-universe, and that something we can only think of as God, a maker of universes, must exist there in some form?'

'It's a possibility,' Leibniz admitted. 'An intriguing one.'

'Humbling?'

'I can emulate pride, but I can't be arsed to feel it,' the Other said, and made Mikhaila suddenly laugh.

There was a short, comfortable silence.

'Think about it,' Mikhaila said. 'There's time. After Homelight...'

'After Homelight,' Leibniz agreed. The Mannequin made a curious gesture with its left hand. 'Then we'll see.'

*

She woke up in the narrow bed feeling disoriented. The room was small and dark, and there were no windows. Mikhaila whispered an order and a soft light came on. She had been dreaming of black holes, and her head felt raw and strange, as if it belonged to someone else.

She sub-vocalized. 'Sandor?'

The reply returned filled with static. 'I'm at the Great Library. I'm glad you finally decided to get up.'

'Did you find anything?'

A pause. Then, 'Meet me at the apex in half an hour?'

She agreed. She got up and prepared genuine coffee from the reproduction-antique coffeemaker provided in her room. Screens around the room woke up to her movements and began showing images of the dark sky as seen from Homelight.

'Pretty,' Leibniz said.

Mikhaila ignored him. She ordered one of the screens and it turned into a mirror. She stood and watched herself, and worried. Her image in the mirror seemed alien to her. Different. An ur-Mikhaila, a stranger wearing her face. The thumb on her left hand was flesh-coloured, only subtly different to the rest of her fingers. She had grafted Leibniz on just before the *Trinity* reached Homelight. Neither of them enjoyed it.

There were dark rings around her eyes. Her breasts felt raw to her, her nipples hurting, and on her ribs, less discreet than the Other, was a patch of red flesh that seemed to crawl on her flat stomach. The Martian bio-construct, its ghost made to sleep.

She kept seeing things from impossible angles. Slivers of light that formed fragmented pictures in her head, familiar images made startling and new.

Alien. She was turning into a fragment herself, something more, or perhaps less, than human. Something *different*. She turned away from the mirror, suddenly uncomfortable with her own naked figure, and dressed quickly before taking hold of the coffee.

Just drinking it was a problem. While the human part of her tasted the coffee, the Other was breaking it down into components, running pointless diagnostics on everything that entered her body. And through the Martian construct the coffee tasted different, a synaesthesia of smells and colours that made her giddy, not helped by the insane dreams of the sleeping ghost riding the interface of flesh.

She didn't finish the coffee. Instead, she opened the door and stepped outside into the corridor. Here was the same level of silence, the same absence of noise: it ran all through the living quarters of the Grand Lodge Pyramid and extended to all its levels, a hush that permeated the air, whispering of mysteries.

Mikhaila thought about the Mysteries as she walked down empty corridors to the service elevators that would take her up to the apex deck with its panorama of desolate views. The conviction that behind the creation of the universe lay God – lay an intelligence, a consciousness, a *something* that made the Big Bang happen, that gave the universe the constants it needed to support life, to create suns and planets and people – was what drove the early Illuminati in the Exodus. It took them on a wild ride through interstellar space, looking for a theoretical hole in the universe, for the tear in space and time where the laws and the constants no longer applied, and where God's eye was open, beyond the universe, watching it in the slow speed of light...

The elevator took her, still within her own bubble of silence, to the apex. She recognized some of the people moving here – new immigrants from Third Eye brought on board the *Trinity* – but the majority were Illuminati scholars, members of the Grand Lodge or the Great Library, identified in the distinguished black robes of the scholars of Mystery.

Sandor was waiting for her beside one of the walls, his gaze lost in the panoramic vista of space and world, and she joined him and watched with him in silence. The green pyramids rose from the surface of Homelight like impossible temples, reaching for the dark night above, and the stars that met her eyes were strangers, the galaxy an unfamiliar ribbon fluttering in the great emptiness.

'We can talk now,' Leibniz said.

Mikhaila turned away from the view and Sandor followed her.

'What did you find?'

Sandor looked tired, and there was a smell about him that took Mikhaila a moment to recognise: dusty paper and mock-leather, the smell of ancient books.

'What I didn't find,' Sandor said. 'There is nothing in the databases about the possibility of life beyond the Eyes. Not even speculation. Not a suggestion, not a theory, nothing.'

'But we knew this,' Mikhaila said. 'My father...'

'Your father,' Sandor wore his unpleasant smile, the one that said he was deeply irritated, 'does not seem to exist. Two papers, both from over thirty years ago, both about nothing in particular.'

Mikhaila stood still, her fingers curling to balls. Then, 'I expected that.'

'Did you?' He looked angry.

'Yes,' Mikhaila muttered, feeling the same anger taking root. 'He always warned me of the possibility. He suspected a conspiracy of the Lodges.'

Sandor laughed, a frustrated bark. 'An Illuminati suspecting a conspiracy. Conspiracies are what we *do*, Mikhaila. Take ten for the price of one. Take your pick. Choose a card, any card.'

'Sandor, calm down,' Leibniz said. He spoke through Mikhaila's mouth, and she felt her body freezing in protest as the Other utilised her vocal cords. The sense of alienation rose in her, threatening to suffocate her. 'We did not expect to find anything in the archives. I've been running duplicate agents on the digital side since we landed. Now what did you find?'

Sandor looked away, drawn back to the view of Homelight beyond the window. 'I found a book.'

'What book?' Leibniz again, silencing Mikhaila's own question.

Sandor laughed again. 'A children's book. From eight hundred years ago. A collection of legends. Everything else is off-limits, or just been borrowed, or doesn't exist, or digitised and destroyed. Guess no one thought there'd be any harm in letting me browse the children's archives.'

Mikhaila felt Leibniz throbbing on her hand, and in the hidden patch below her own robe the Martian bio-construct stirred, the ghost inside it trying to wake up. She felt both of the influences like sharp, medical pains, and a phantom smell of spirits tickled her nose. '*What* book?'

'*The Legend of Aldus Trismegistus.*'

Mikhaila stilled. The name, dimly familiar, evoked in her a certain dread that she could feel pumping up from her abdomen. And the ghost was nearly roused now, the name of the book acting as a drug on its fragile consciousness. She felt Leibniz's reaction even before he spoke. 'Who was Aldus Trismegistus and what was the manner of his death?' Then she remembered.

It was an old riddle, a children's nursery rhyme, learnt on the playground, separated from her now by both space and time.

'He was a man,' Sandor said, 'who entered a joining with an Other. He slept...'

'For a thousand years,' Mikhaila said, remembering. 'As the ships left Earth system and went searching for God. And he was woken up only when the First Eye was found, and then...'

'He killed himself. *Them*selves. Three-times Aldus, who joined with an Other, and merged with a Martian aug. He threw himself into First Eye, three thousand years ago. That's what the book tells.'

'And?' Mikhaila wanted to know. A headache was blossoming inside her, and the ghost was whispering to her, dribbling of sex and the flesh and something else too: an old memory of childhood and of singing an even older rhyme.

'And that's it,' Sandor answered. 'In the nursery rhyme.'

'But not in the book.'

'No.' The word was flat and heavy, like an old, forgotten tombstone. 'You see, the book doesn't end with Aldus' death. In the story, Aldus never died at all.'

'He still lives,' Leibniz said. 'Is that it?' But Mikhaila already knew he was right, and she took control over her vocal cords and said, 'He went into the Eye, but he didn't die–' and the old rhyme returned to her, like a persistent shard of music, and she saw in Sandor's eye the same wild thought as he completed the words: '-Aldus Trismegistus was one and three times alive.'

*

There were words expressing sorrow at her loss, quiet warnings about the futility of hope, words of advice about grieving and letting go of the dead. The room, high up on the Southern corner of the Grand Lodge Pyramid, twinkled with light; a fine mist fell from the high ceiling onto lush, transparent vegetation of a kind she had never seen before. Designer plants, sucking up the mist and turning all the colours of the rainbow.

'Your father was a good man,' Grand Master Rune said to her, his hand enveloping a rolled crystal leaf containing an amber drink. 'He would be proud of you. You did good to come here and bring us the new immigrants. You're a true Illuminati, Mikhaila. Remember we must all serve.'

Grand Master Rune was short and hairless, his head a shaven dome. His eyes were deep-set and ordinary brown. His fingers were bitten, the skin around the nails raw and red. Earlier he said, 'We were initiated together, your father and I. I was sorry to hear of the accident.'

The words of the old riddle still echoed in her head. 'Who was Aldus Trismegistus and how did he die?' She felt it reverberating through her new components. The Martian aug crawled across her stomach and wrapped itself around a breast, shivering. She was going insane; or perhaps, she thought, not sure which part of her the thought came from, she was becoming Aldus.

'You don't look well,' Rune remarked, and he released his drink into the air, the leaf unfurling and sailing away on an invisible breeze. His gaze took her in, all of her: she saw him note the Other on her hand and his eyes lingered for longer than necessary on her breasts, as if knowing there was something alien there that did not belong.

Or maybe, she thought, he's just looking at your tits.

'Sit down,' he said. He guided her away from the throngs of people to a quiet corner. Two giant leaves unfolded from a stem and they sat down, the leaves moulding themselves around their bodies. 'Mikhaila,' he began, and his voice abandoned its mere-human tones and took on the aspect of a Grand Master, stern and impersonal and powerful. 'Whatever you are doing to yourself, don't. Do not meddle with things you do not understand.'

Mikhaila tried to smile. 'I'm an Illuminati,' she said. 'It's what we *do*.'

The Grand Master shook his head in an old gesture of negation. 'You are not high up enough in the study of the Mysteries. Don't go seeking conspiracies where none exist. Look at you.' He gestured to Leibniz, but the gesture seemed to take in more than that, hinting at the Martian biomass and its ghostly rider. 'You're killing yourself.'

'Like Aldus Trismegistus?' Mikhaila wanted to know, feeling a sense of relief as the words were out, a challenge. Time to put down your cards, she thought.

Rune blinked. She noticed his own discreet Martian aug, a faint red line running down his neck, behind his ear. And he too, she saw, had an Other, though this one was in his left earlobe and was so discreet she had to know it was there to see it. 'If you like.'

'What would you have me do?' Mikhaila asked. 'Tell me the truth. Tell me why Third Eye is becoming inhospitable. Tell me why I was not allowed to study the Eye. Tell me...' The thought remained unformed in speech.

Tell me why my father died.

'Go home,' Rune said instead. 'Say goodbye to your father. Mikhaila,' he paused, and then said, 'the Grand Lodge has been concerned for some time – for several hundred years in fact – with the possibility that life this close to the Eyes might become even more dangerous.' He turned to her and his eyes took hers in, forcing her to pay him attention. 'We have decided to organise ... an expedition. For the first time in two millennia, we would like to expand – and to re-establish contact with other parts of humanity, if any exist in the direction we once came from.'

Mikhaila drew in breath, imagining the oxygen rushing through her bloodstream, cleansing her. She felt her pulse race up despite the air she was inhaling. Leibniz warned her, *sotto voce*, to be careful.

'As one of our finest starship captains,' the Grand Master said, and for the first time since she met him Rune smiled, 'we would like you and the *Trinity* to be a part of the expedition.'

Mikhaila found she was unable to speak. She felt a fever rise in her and the voices of her body's co-habitants threatened to drown her own thoughts, which were of journeys and strangeness and adventure.

'Think about it,' Rune urged her. He rose and the leaf he was sitting on furled back on itself. 'But go home first. Your aunt misses you.'

He walked away, but Mikhaila remained sitting, and all the while Leibniz was whispering to her about bribes, and about carrots and sticks.

*

The fever burned her. Her body had become a battle-ground, a clash of entities too alien to co-exist. The Martian *thing* was tight around her waist and seemed to be spreading, growing over her stomach and breasts. And the ghost that haunted it was fully awake now, and insane. Its jabbering hurt her like thousands of internal cuts.

Leibniz kept quiet. The Other throbbed where her thumb had been, as if barricading himself against the mayhem in her body, though with little success. Her mind became a screen where sequences of different and alien codes clashed and competed, a miniature breeding ground of Human and Martian and Other.

When she gained partial consciousness she felt she was on fire, the bedsheets heavy with sweat, and she caught snatches of conversation as if from far away. She heard Sandor talking about carrots and sticks, and understood from what he said that at some point before leaving Homelight the *Trinity's* systems had been carefully wiped of the Hawking Radiation data they had collected at Third Eye. Rochiro seemed completely upset about this invasion of her domain, more than she seemed at Mikhaila's condition. Sandor spoke in short angry bursts and Rochiro was a sequence of longer notes against him.

When she dreamed she saw evolutions. She went through condensed minutes of Martian evolution as it may have been, the alien genetic code producing an ecology of stunning complexity; and she dreamed the ghost's dreams, in which she walked through an ancient temple and schemed to become Uploaded, and saw shadows wherever she turned.

She felt herself changing. Somewhere inside her codes began to match, to mutate into each other. To communicate.

The fever burned her. She felt as if she was no longer human. And when the voices in her head merged at last into one, she knew what she had to do.

*

She no longer needed the erased data. As they approached First Eye, the heaviest and largest of the three black holes the Illuminati had discovered at the end of their immensely long journey, her new eyes began to see the quantum radiation leaking and her new mind was on the verge of deciphering it.

It was...strange. As if a mathematics that felt somehow wrong had become a series of deferred signifiers, operating within an exotic Saussurean *language*. She couldn't comprehend it; but gradually she began to discern places where the alien nature of the code abated, became almost human. She began listening for those moments, for their rhythm as they trickled out of the Eye like tears.

When Mikhaila woke up the *Trinity* was already decelerating towards First Eye and her aunt was demanding that she speak to her. It had been seven years since she had been home; though to her it was only a year. She made a good impression of the old Mikhaila and told her aunt that she needed time alone.

Then she took her Cyclop and stole away from the *Trinity*.

She floated alone and invisible, the black hole a piece of darkness in a universe of stars, and she listened to it talk.

She thought she could hear her father's voice, sometimes, in between the too-alien code. She thought he said her name, but she couldn't be sure.

She could hear other voices too. She thought she heard her mother, who was sent into the Eye when Mikhaila was only a girl. She remembered the day of the funeral, the way her father almost didn't cry.

She thought about the idea they had come up with, this small group of Illuminati *within* Illuminati: that life may have evolved beyond the Eye's event horizon, in that relative band of stable space-time. A kind of life that sat inside God's eye, caught between a universe they could only see and a place where the world ended. All matter is information, her father had said, all matter is data. We always thought we went straight to God, but maybe there's a stop on the way.

There was only one way to know. The Cyclop rode the pull of the Eye, heading lazily towards the massive gravity well. Mikhaila hardly paid attention, she was listening so hard. It was like reading signals in the sand, wiped away too quickly by the rushing water.

She thought she felt the tides as they began to pull her body apart, but when she looked outside she saw it was a sleek dark ship and that it was forcing her to it. She could have cried.

She *almost* understood the message. She felt her eyes growing heavy as she approached the ship, and then she blacked out.

*

She knew something was being done to her, both to her body and to her mind. A breaking up. A separation. She felt the moment the Otherness was gone, felt Leibniz as he was re-formed beside her, a lone and separate entity. After a while she could no longer feel the ghost, and when she woke up and looked down at herself all that remained of the blind Martian construct were pale bands of skin, like bars across her chest and stomach. She woke up grieving. It was a defeat. She had hoped for transcendence, and she had failed.

Gradually she began to recognise the images that were coming through her eyes, though her seeing felt limited, singular and uneasy. The first thing she saw was Aunt Alexandra's face. The Grand Mistress was looking down on her with a frown. Mikhaila began to form a word but couldn't and her aunt's face changed: an expression of concern that touched Mikhaila unexpectedly.

She slept, and didn't dream.

When she woke up her aunt was there again.

'You were being driven mad,' Aunt Alexandra explained to her. Mikhaila was trying to sit up and finding it difficult. 'How could you think of jumping into a black hole before it's your time?'

'What have you got to hide?' Mikhaila demanded, the words coming slow and unfamiliar. 'That something lives inside? That we could *talk* to it?'

'Yes,' her aunt said, 'something lives inside.' And this sudden admission, most of all, lifted away an old weight in Mikhaila's mind and made her light-headed.

'But can we talk to it?" her aunt asked. "To them? You tried, and you were ready to kill yourself.'

'I would have ... lived inside,' Mikhaila whispered. Her eyes wouldn't focus. 'All matter is information. They would have re-built me, like they did my

119

father.'

'Mikhaila...' Aunt Alexandra looked into her eyes and sighed. 'You think there are ghosts beyond the event horizon? The Illuminati dead risen in heaven? You tried to understand them – they, it, whatever we can try and call whatever is inside there – and even augmented as you were in the strands of three evolutions you failed. The simple truth is we don't understand what's behind the event horizon but we treat it with respect – and with caution.'

'It's a conspiracy,' Mikhaila said, but discovered that she couldn't feel much about it. She remembered the children's book Sandor had discovered and it nearly made her smile. 'Is that why Aldus Trismegistus died? Is that the answer to the riddle?'

'No,' another voice declared. '*That* was a story.' The face of a man appeared beside her aunt. No, not a man. An avatar. 'I managed to control my three components. I was two centuries older than you back then. And a time came when the human and Martian parts of me remained only in their pure code, and I migrated almost entirely into my Other body.' He paused. 'But I never died.'

'Three-times Aldus, who joined with an Other, and merged with a Martian aug,' Mikhaila half sang, and found that, though she didn't know why, she believed him.

'The song got it wrong,' the avatar said, a little stiffly. 'Aldus was the Other. The name of the human was Scott.'

Aunt Alexandra coughed. 'You can consider yourself initiated into the Greater Mysteries as of now,' she said. 'You know almost as much as we do. I tried to tell my brother to wait and that he wasn't ready, but he didn't listen. He did the same thing as you, and it drove him insane. Is he there? Sometimes I think he is. I listen to the Eye and I can almost hear him talking to me. But if he is, then he is too alien now. Since Aldus's time we did a lot of research on three-way interfaces. I'm ... changed. Perhaps too much. But it isn't working. It isn't enough.'

Mikhaila thought of the way she was driven towards the Eye. Was that what happened to her father? She tried to remember back, looking for signs: he must have already been augmented before she left. And she thought, he must have dealt with Alvarez.

She felt chilled now, having experienced that same painful imperfect joining. Did he have marks on his skin? Was he wearing long clothes? She thought he did but could no longer be sure.

'We need something more, Mikhaila,' Aldus said. 'We need another element. Another way of seeing. Another form of life. That's why we're sending out the starships. Not to go back, but to go further.' The avatar's eyes were almond-shaped, a too-detailed reproduction of a human eye. 'To find new life, and join with them.'

'That's enough,' Aunt Alexandra cut in. 'She needs to rest.'

Aldus looked at her and inclined his head. 'Sleep well,' he said, 'Grandmistress.'

Mikhaila, head suddenly full of starships and stars, let herself close her eyes at the words, and sleep claimed her immediately. Her dreams felt lighter, belonging to her alone; for she knew now that, whatever happened, she was once more herself, and the memories receded. She only dreamed, a dream that would in the coming years recur to her: that she was floating, a being of peace, and a child of pure light, shining into the watching God's eyes.

CONTRIBUTORS

Chris Butler has had stories published in *Asimov's*, *Interzone* and other outlets. His novel, *Any Time Now*, was published by Cosmos Books in 2001. He lives on the south coast of England. His story, "Have Guitar, Will Travel," appears here for the first time.

Colin P Davies is a writer and illustrator whose work has seen publication in venues such as *Asimov's*, *Bewildering*, *Spectrum SF* and others. His story, "Dolls," first appeared in issue two of *3SF*. It is reprinted here with permission.

Aliette de Bodard is a Campbell award finalist and a winner of the Writers of the Future award. She lives and works in Paris. Her work has appeared in *Interzone*, *Black Static*, *Realms of Fantasy*, *Beneath Ceaseless Skies*, and other venues. Her first novel, *Servant of the Underworld*, is available from Angry Robot, an imprint of Harper Collins. Her story, "Father's Last Ride," appears here for the first time.

Tanith Lee is a preeminent master of the field. Over the years, her stories have seen publication in venues too numerous to list and her work has been anthologized multiple times. Tanith is the author of at least fifty-four novels—at last count, anyway—including the *Paradys Cycle* of books and the *Wolf Tower Sequence*. She has won or been nominated for the Nebula and the World Fantasy award several times over. Her story, "Tan," appears here for the first time.

Jason Erik Lundberg is an American ex-patriot living in Singapore. His stories have appeared in *The Daily Cabal*, *Sybil's Garage*, *The Quarterly Literary Review Singapore*, with work forthcoming from *Polyphony 7*, *Subterranean* and many others. His story,

"The Time Traveler's Son," was originally published by Papaveria Press in 2008 and is reprinted here by permission.

Gareth Owens has had stories published in *Nature, Mallorn: The Journal of the Tolkien Society, Ruins: Terra (anthology,* Hadley Rille Books, 2007*), The West Pier Gazette and Other Stories (*anthology, Three Legged Fox Books, 2007*),* and others. He is a writer resident on the south coast of England. His story, "Mango Dictionary and the Dragon Queen of Contract Evolution," has appeared in his collection *Fun With Rainbows* (Immersion Press, 2010) and is reprinted here with permission.

Al Robertson is a London based writer whose works have seen published in *The Third Alternative, Postscripts 17, Midnight Street, Interzone,* and many others. Al's story, "Golden," was originally published in issue thirty-eight of *The Third Alternative*. It is reprinted here with permission.

Gord Sellar is an American ex-patriot living in South Korea. His stories have appeared in such places as *Subterranean, Asimov's, Fantasy Magazine, Clarkesworld, Apex Digest* and others. He has been given an honorable mention on more than one occasion in *The Years Best Science Fiction,* edited by Gardner Dozois. His story, "The Broken Pathway," is printed here for the first time.

Anne Stringer is editor for the acclaimed publication known as *Murky Depths.* She is also co-founder of the award-winning podcast, Variant Frequencies. Her work has appeared in both print, e-zine and podcast form. Anne's story, "Grave Robbers," appears here for the first time.

Eric James Stone has seen publication in various outlets, including *Apex Digest, Analog, Intergalactic Medicine Show,* and *Jim Baen's Universe.* A winner in the Writer's of the Future Contest, 2004, he resides in Utah where he works as a web developer. His story, "Bird-Dropping and Sunday," appears here for the first time.

Lavie Tidhar is an eclectic writer who calls the world his home. His life spent on a kibbutz in Israel, time spent in South Africa, the UK, Asia and remote islands in the south Pacific have clearly shaped his worldview and his fiction. His work has appeared in *Interzone, Apex Digest, Fantasy Magazine, Clarkesworld, Strange Horizons* and selected anthologies. His story, "Lode Stars," appears here for the first time.